CHEMISTRY

CHEMISTRY

A NOVEL

Weike Wang

ALFRED A. KNOPF   New York

2017

THIS IS A BORZOI BOOK
PUBLISHED BY ALFRED A. KNOPF

Copyright © 2017 by Weike Wang

Grateful acknowledgment is made to Hal Leonard LLC for
permission to reprint a lyric excerpt from "Don't Stop Me Now,"
words and music by Freddie Mercury. Copyright © 1978 by
Queen Music Ltd. All rights administered by Sony/ATV Music
Publishing LLC. International copyright secured. All rights
reserved. Reprinted by permission of Hal Leonard LLC.

Knopf, Borzoi Books, and the colophon are registered trademarks
of Penguin Random House LLC.

A portion of this work orginally appeared, in different form,
in *Ploughshares* (Summer 2016).

ISBN 978-1-5247-3174-8

Jacket design by Janet Hansen

Manufactured in the United States of America

Epigraph (*mathematics, noun*):

the set of all points lying on or above a function's graph

PART I

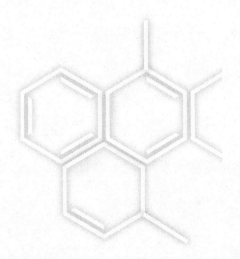

PART I

The boy asks the girl a question. It is a question of marriage. Ask me again tomorrow, she says, and he says, That's not how this works.

Diamond is no longer the hardest mineral known to man. *New Scientist* reports that lonsdaleite is. Lonsdaleite is 58 percent harder than diamond and forms only when meteorites smash themselves into Earth.

. . .

The lab mate says to make a list of pros and cons.

Write it all down, prove it to yourself.

She then nods sympathetically and pats me on the arm.

The lab mate is a solver of hard problems. Her desk is next to mine but is neater and more result-producing.

Big deal, she says of her many, many publications and doesn't take herself too seriously, is busy but not that busy, talks about things other than chemistry.

I find her outlook refreshing, yet strange. If I were that accomplished, I would casually bring up my published papers in conversation. Have you read so-and-so? Because it is quite worth your time. The tables alone are beautiful and well formatted.

I have only one paper out. The tables are in fact very beautiful, all clear and double-spaced line borders. All succinct and informative titles.

Somewhere I read that the average number of readers for a scientific paper is 0.6.

So I make the list. The pros are extensive.

Eric cooks dinner. Eric cooks great dinners. Eric hands me the toothbrush with toothpaste on it and sometimes even sticks it in my mouth. Eric takes out the trash, the recycling; waters all our plants because I can't seem to remember that they're living things. These leaves feel crunchy, he said after the week that he was gone.

He goes that week to California for a conference with other young and established chemists.

Also Eric drives me to lab when it's too rainy to bike. Boston sees a great deal of rain. Sometimes the rain comes down horizontal and hits the face.

Also Eric walks the dog. We have a dog. Eric got him for me.

I realize that I don't have any cons. I knew this going in.

It is a half-list, I tell the lab mate the next day, and she offers to buy me a cookie.

In lab, there are two boxes filled with argon. It is where I do highly sensitive chemistry, the kind that can never see air. Once air is let in, the chemicals catch fire. It is also where I wish to put my head on days of nothing going right.

On those days, I add the wrong amount of catalyst. Or I add the wrong catalyst.

Catalysts make reactions go faster. They lower activation energy, which is the indecision each reaction faces before committing to its path.

What use is this work in the long run? I ask myself in the room when I am alone. The solvent room officially, but I have renamed it the Fortress of Solitude.

Eric is no longer in this lab. He graduated last year and is now in another lab. A chemistry PhD takes at least five years to complete. We met when I was in my first and he was in his second.

Now I walk around our apartment and trip over his stuff: big black drum bags and steel pots and carboys with brown liquid fermenting inside. Eric plays the drums and brews beer. One con is how much space these two hobbies take up, but this is outweighed by the drums that I like to hear and the beer that I like to drink.

My pro list grows at an exponential rate.

. . .

We had talked about marriage before. Can you see yourself settling down, having kids? Can you see yourself starting a family? I didn't say no, but I didn't say yes. We had these talks casually. Each time, he thought if actually proposed to, I would say something different.

At least now all my cards are on the table, he says. But please don't take too long to decide.

. . .

It has been the summer of unbearable heat. At the Home Depot, we go up and down aisles looking for a fan. Our last fan broke yesterday and next week it is supposed to be hotter. Then next month, a hurricane.

When Eric sees the hurricane report, he wonders if the people who wrote it are just screwing with us.

Why would they do that? I ask.

Because it's funny.

Oh, right. Then a minute later, I laugh.

Patience is Eric's greatest virtue. He will wait in longer lines than I will and think nothing of it. He will smile, while holding a heavy fan, at the older woman in front of him who has brought a tall stack of lampshades and at the moment of payment is having second thoughts. She asks the clerk for his opinion. She asks Eric. Do I need the magenta? Me, she doesn't bother with, because I am the one with the furiously tapping foot. The woman considers some more, turning each lampshade in her hands, but in the end purchases nothing.

I tell Eric in the car that if I were to reimagine Hell, it would be no different from the line we were just in. Except the woman would never decide on a lampshade and the line would never move.

Can you imagine? I say. A worse punishment than pushing that thing up the hill.

A boulder, Eric says.

I realize what a hypocrite I'm being, to make him wait for an answer and then dwell on a twenty-five-minute line.

Once home, Eric sets the fan up and the dog goes crazy.

. . .

Two years ago, Eric and I moved in together. We do not have a dog but we are thinking about it. What kind? Eric asks. Big? Small? I don't have a preference. How about just adorable?

When he first brings him home, I hear the tail, long and bushy, thumping against the couch. A forty-five-pound goldendoodle. Incredibly adorable. When he runs, his ears flop. If we never groomed him, his hair would keep growing and he would look like a blond bear.

The blond bear loves people and this is good. But then we discover that he is afraid of everything else: the hair dryer, an empty box, the fan.

. . .

Bad tempers run in my family. It is the dominant allele, like black hair. Eric has red hair. Our friends have asked if there is any way our babies will turn out to be gingers. Gingers are dying out, and our friends are concerned about Eric's beautiful locks.

I say, Unless Mendel was completely wrong about genetics, our babies will have my hair.

But our friends can still dream. An Asian baby with red hair. One friend says, You could write a *Science* paper on that and then apply for academic jobs and then get tenure.

Eric is already looking for academic jobs. He wants to teach at a college that primarily serves undergrads.

Because they are the future, he says. Eager to learn, energetic, and happy, more or less, as compared with grad students. With undergrads, I can make a real difference.

I don't say this but I think it: You are the only person I know who talks like that. So enthusiastically and benefit-of-the-doubt-giving.

But the colleges he's interested in are not in Boston. They are in places like Oberlin, Ohio.

I am certain that Eric will get the job. His career path is very straight, like that of an arrow to its target. If I were to draw my path out, it would look like a gas particle flying around in space.

The lab mate often echoes the wisdom of many chemists before her. You must love chemistry even when it is not working. You must love chemistry unconditionally.

The friends who ask about the red-haired babies are the ones recently married or the ones recently married with a dog. Whenever we have them over for dinner, like tonight, they think we are trying to tell them that we are engaged.

News? they say.

Not yet, I reply, but here, have some freshly grated Parmesan cheese instead.

Behind my back, I know they are less kind. They ask each other, It's been four years, hasn't it? They joke, She is only with him for his money.

It is common knowledge now that graduate students make close to nothing and that there are more PhD scientists in this country than there are jobs for them.

When Eric first decides to do a PhD, it is in high school. He takes a chemistry class and excels. This is in western Maryland, in a town with many steepled churches but no Starbucks. Every other year we drive three hours from the DC airport, through a gap in the Appalachian Mountains, and arrive at a picturesque place where Eric seems to know everyone. He waves to the man across the horseshoe bar, his former band teacher. He waves to the woman at the post office, the mother of a high school friend. The diner with the horseshoe bar is called Niners. There is always farm-land for sale and working mills.

Sometimes I wonder why he left a place where every ice-cream shop is called a creamery to work seventy-hour weeks in lab. He credits the chemistry teacher, who asked him often, What are you going to do afterward? And don't just say stick around.

. . .

A belief among Chinese mothers is that children pick their own traits in the womb. The smart ones work diligently to pick the better traits. The dumb ones get easily flustered and fall asleep. For their laziness, they are then dealt the worse traits.

Or perhaps this is just a belief of my own mother.

Had you chosen better, you would have not ended up with your father's terrible temper or my poor vision.

I don't want to believe this but it has become so ingrained. Compared with mine, Eric's temper is nonexistent.

Thursday, trash day. We pick the wrong streets to

go down and drive for miles behind a garbage truck. It is a one-way road. It is also a one-lane road. But not once does he sigh or complain. He puts on jazz music instead. Listen to this, he says. But all I hear is the going and stopping of the truck, the picking up and dumping of trash, the clanking of metal bins. So frustrated am I after one song that I lean over and press the horn for him. Then out the window, I shout at the truck, Excuse me, do you mind?

·   ·   ·

The PhD advisor visits my desk, sits down, brings his hands together, and asks, Where do you see your project going in five years?

Five years? I say in disbelief. I would hope to be graduated by then and in the real world with a job.

I see, he says. Perhaps then it is time to start a new project, one that is more within your capabilities.

He leaves me to it.

The desire to throw something at his head never goes away. Depending on what he says, it is either the computer or the desk.

I sketch out possible projects. Alchemy, for one. If I could achieve that today, I could graduate tomorrow.

A guy in lab strongly believes that women do not belong in science. He's said that women lack the balls to actually do science.

Which isn't wrong. We do lack balls.

But if he had said that to me at the start of grad

school, I would have punched him. Coming in, I think myself the best at chemistry. In high school, I win a national award for it. I say, cockily, at orientation, Yes, that was me, only to realize that everyone else had won it as well, at some point, in addition to awards I have never won.

The lab guy is still around. He works with the lab mate. If all goes well, they will have another paper next year and then they will graduate.

Women lack the balls to do science, he still says. With the exception of your lab mate. She has three.

Later I ask Eric, How many balls do you think I have?

It is poor timing. We have just gotten into bed and started to kiss.

Uh, none? he says, and the kissing is over. I was hoping he would have said something along the lines of three and a half.

.   .   .

A Chinese proverb: Outside of sky there is sky, outside of people there are people.

It is the idea of infinity and also that there will always be someone better than you.

Eric says the proverb reminds him of a story from Indian philosophy.

Three hundred years ago, the world was believed to be a flat plate that rested on an elephant that rested on a turtle. Below that turtle was another turtle and below that turtle was another one. It was turtles all the way down.

. . .

I call the best friend whenever I can. She is a doctor in Manhattan. Her husband, a businessman. Together they have money, a housekeeper, and a midtown condo, twelve stories up in the air.

Compared with my other friends, they are the longest married, having married right out of college and then continued onward in their careers.

At the time, they decide this way is best, logistically, because she does not think she will have time to plan a wedding in medical school or residency. And what if residency ruins this figure, she says on her wedding day, a hand on her flat stomach, in the room where I am helping her dress.

She is a beautiful bride. Residency ruins nothing.

I have known this girl since third grade. We grow up in adjacent Michigan towns and meet through family friends. I don't know her that well before I know this—by second grade, she has taken an interest in rubber cement. She likes to pour it on her hands and lick it off.

Now she tells her patients to stop eating trans fats for the sake of their clogged arteries and, thoughtfully, prescribes drugs. Let me give you a checkup, she says whenever I call, and I must vehemently decline. Not because I doubt her skill but because I have seen her eat rubber cement.

That was a long time ago, she says.

Yes, but who knows what the long-term effects are. No one has ever studied them.

What's this about your chemistry? she says today. Why isn't it going well? You put in the hours, then how is it that you get nothing?

The way I have explained it is through LEGOs. The chemistry that I do involves putting many LEGOs together and having another LEGO come out. The LEGOs are molecules, but unlike real LEGOs, I cannot see them or touch them.

I am a senior in college when I decide to go into synthetic organic chemistry. I am mesmerized by the art of it. The purpose of this kind of chemistry is to build a molecule that is already present in nature, but to build it better than nature, in the least number of steps, with a beautiful key step. Technique is everything. Percent yield is everything. For months I am running the same reaction over and over again, the seventh step of a twenty-four-step synthesis, just so I can get the yield up from 50 percent to 65 because anything under 60 is unacceptable to the advisor. Then for months, I am running step eight. Then for years, the advisor is asking, Do we have it, the molecule? And I say, No, it is still at large.

In time, you find yourself no longer mesmerized.

I do not always like talking to the best friend about my work.

She sometimes starts to say, Well, when I was in orgo lab, I remember it being fine. Don't LEGOs come with a manual?

And this makes me a little mad.

Once I finish writing it, they will hand me a PhD.

Your orgo lab was for a class. You had a partner. The experiments you were asked to do were supposed to work. You weren't trying to discover anything new.

Okay, okay, she says.

Out of the blue, she asks if I have been writing anything else.

Like what?

I don't know. Didn't you used to write things?

That was a long time ago, I say.

In college, I took some writing classes and for one semester thought, If this wasn't so blatantly impractical, I would go into writing.

An ideal world: money falls from the sky and into my lap for each word that I write. A one-dollar flat rate. A twenty for a real zinger.

. . .

I am an only child, and so is Eric. This is not a deal breaker, but it does make me fear for our future.

Imagine two only children marrying, staying together, and then our parents getting sick. Imagine us flying out to see these parents, four in total if they get sick at the same time, as Murphy's Law would allow, and only two of us. Imagine if we have children, how many people we would have to see and tend to. And then who would walk the dog?

If this dog dies from neglect, I will never forgive myself.

Eric has mixed feelings about being an only child.

This is because he has a family that loves him too much. From kindergarten to sixth grade, his mother puts handwritten notes in his lunch box. She writes things like *You are my sun and stars.*

That's sweet, I say, until I think more about the phrase.

You cannot be two things at once: You are not light, both wave and particle. You are not Schrödinger's cat, both dead and alive.

Flip over the note and find a Spider-Man sticker to be put on a hand or a lunch box that's already covered in stickers.

In sixth grade, Eric finally writes back to this mother, *Please stop writing me notes and sending me stickers. You're embarrassing me in front of everyone.*

I meet his entire family at his thesis defense. Mother, father, aunts and uncles, both sets of grandparents. They sit in the back row and stand up after he has finished, not having understood anything but cheering wildly.

At his celebratory dinner, one after the other, they offer him questions.

How does it feel to be the most successful one in the

family? How does it feel to be the smartest one in the family?

Are they joking? No, they are being sincere. I stop eating at the word *brilliant*.

His family does not all live in that picturesque town but close by. One week, there is a picnic. Another, a family barbecue. I suspect this is the real reason he leaves. All that attention can be suffocating, he now says. But what does he experience when he first comes to the city for a PhD? Isolation? Shock? No, he is incredibly happy. He thrives.

I find a story like that hard to believe. Maybe this is why I ask, What is the worst thing your parents have ever said to you? What is the worst thing you have ever seen them do?

He is taken aback. He thinks for a long time. When he comes up empty-handed I say, There must have been a moment when you realized the meanness of a parent, and the look he gives me is the one that says this is not a competition, our upbringings, this is not up for discussion.

So I shut up.

.   .   .

How do you predict things like angst and risky behavior? How do you predict things like ungrateful- ness? We've mapped the entire human genome but don't know what most of it says. And then the other problems—heart disease, cancer, poor vision.

When I watch that movie *Gattaca,* I think, What a perfect society, to build your own child, what a great idea.

DNA unzips to replicate and undergo meiosis, to make things like egg and sperm that come together to make things like babies.

It is this unzipping that I find sensual. It is like the unzipping of a woman's dress.

.   .   .

In Arizona, a PhD advisor dies. Authorities blame the grad student who shot him, but grad students around the world blame the advisor. No student can graduate without the advisor's approval. This advisor had kept the student in lab for seventeen years, believing him too valuable to be let go or simply having gone insane. I think, Kudos to the student for making it to seventeen years. I would have shot someone at ten.

My advisor is more reasonable than that, which is why he is still alive. His door is always open. He visits my desk often, asking for results and, if I do not have any, asking if I am unwell.

I'm fine, I say.

Your lab mate is working steadily, he says. She comes in on weekends and holidays. Have you been doing the same?

Not really. Not Christmas or Thanksgiving. Or the time I was bedridden with the flu.

My advisor has never shaken his head at me, but he won't smile.

If alchemy doesn't work, I will move on to desalinating all of our oceans and providing freshwater to the people.

.   .   .

In traditional Chinese culture, the bride gets married in red. The dress is called a *qipao*. It is very slimming, with capped sleeves, a high collar, and a button in the middle of that collar that sits in the valley between the clavicles.

Last summer, I pass a *qipao* store that says FREE FITTING. I am in Chinatown buying cake. It is Eric's birthday and sponge cake can be bought no place else. The *qipao* store I have never noticed before. Should I go in? I hesitate but the seamstress at the door is very convincing. Every *qipao* on sale, every *qipao* under fifty dollars. Silk. Handmade. Just try. Take five minutes. I don't believe any of this but then she adds that I look very skinny from afar.

The woman makes clear that the *qipao* is not for anyone who is fat. She says, If you're fat, wear an A-line.

But after putting the dress on, I realize that the fit is not for me. I don't have the shoulders for it.

Too broad, she says, and horizontal. She keeps trying to push them down with both hands.

I learn from this woman that the *qipao* is not entirely Chinese, not Han Chinese, which is the majority ethnic group in China, which is what I am. It actually came from the Manchurians in the north, who are known for their excellent archery while riding horseback across the great northern plains.

I learn from this woman that the *qipao* is not even a wedding dress. It is simply a traditional dress, for any occasion.

Yet I don't remember either my mother or grandmother wearing one. Quickly I realize something. While beautiful, the *qipao* is hard to walk in, the legs bound together, the fabric constricting, the slit up to the mid-thigh.

In the end, I buy the dress anyway. I can't see myself in the red and choose a deep burgundy color. Though don't ask me how many times I've worn it.

.　.　.

See how red clashes with your skin tone, my mother says, putting her pale arm up against mine. She does this often, especially when I am a teenager.

You have your father's skin, dark and swarthy, fitting if you were to live in the countryside and blend in with the soil.

My mother grows up in Shanghai, in an apartment building with a terrace overlooking the Bund. It is the mid-1970s and she is thirteen, watching from this terrace shipping boats with large quilted sails come through the Huangpu River. The Pudong skyline is not what it will be in twenty years. The Oriental Pearl Tower will not be built until 1994. There are few cars and buses on the road, but there are thousands of bikes. The youngest of two, my mother does not always like going to school or learning but she does every dare her brother tells her, like scale this wall in your best dress, like stack all the dinner bowls into a pyramid. She scales the wall and ruins her dress. She stacks the bowls and breaks every one. But she is rarely ever punished. She is a beautiful girl with large eyes and everyone tells her so.

My father grows up hundreds of miles west of Shanghai. There are no buildings taller than a story. There are no bikes. It is farm country and he is the oldest of seven. His father is a farmer and so is his grandfather. They grow wheat, sorghum, corn, and sell them in the city. But food is scarce in the household and there is strict rationing. No child has a second serving of anything. No child has more than two sets of clothes at one time. The house they live in is small, too small, and he shares a bedroom with all six of his siblings. Things like glass windows and wooden doors are expensive, so the house has neither. The door is an opening covered with a thin cloth. The window, another opening but not covered. At dawn and dusk, my father is studying. Whenever he does not have to be in the field, he is studying.

How do they meet? Fall in love? All good questions. The story changes every time. They meet through mutual friends. They meet accidentally, at a train station, at a bus station, no, on a bridge. Though neither of them remembers the exact date of this meeting.

And then they are married. And then they have me.

My father's is the classic immigrant story.

He is the first in his family to go to high school and college and graduate school and America. He is the first to become an engineer.

Extraordinary, some people have said when he speaks now of how he got here.

Through hard work, he says, and the learning of advanced math.

Amazing, others have said.

But such progress he's made in one generation that to progress beyond him, I feel as if I must leave America and colonize the moon.

·   ·   ·

Genetics aside, I don't see myself having kids.

Not one? Eric asks.

If I had one, I would want to have two, and if I had two, I would want to have zero.

·   ·   ·

An object in motion stays in motion; an object at rest stays at rest.

Where is Eric today?

In motion. He makes lists of places where he is going to apply. He applies.

I glance at the first draft of his application essay, at the first sentence that describes his love of teaching, and lightly, with a pencil, cross out the word *love*.

Afterward, I can't even explain to him why I did that.

The hurricane they said would come never does. Having boarded up her windows already, the best friend is now disappointed. She says, If doctors were wrong as often as weathermen, we would all be fired. Imagine if I told you that you had a 90 percent chance of diabetes and then you never got it. Wouldn't you be pissed?

I would probably be more relieved. Then I remind her that rain and diabetes are not really the same things.

Instead of the hurricane, fall arrives early. On the first cold day, I walk outside and gasp at the sight of my breath.

.   .   .

A Chinese proverb predicts that for every man with great skill, there is a woman with great beauty.

In ancient China, there are four great beauties:

The first so beautiful that when fish see her reflection they forget how to swim and sink.

The second so beautiful that birds forget how to fly and fall.

The third so beautiful that the moon refuses to shine.

The fourth so beautiful that flowers refuse to bloom.

I find it interesting how often beauty is shown to make the objects around it feel worse.

This proverb is said and re-said on the day of my parents' wedding.

Throughout her twenties, my mother is complimented wildly. People stop her in the streets and say, You remind me of an actress from a movie. That actress is Audrey Hepburn from *Roman Holiday*.

She likes this movie. The scene where the hand goes into the mouth of the statue—it is like a dare her brother would have had her do.

Most people feel that beauty is not in the face but in the heart or the soul or the mind—any place that the human eye cannot penetrate is where beauty will hide.

Most people say that I look nothing like my mother and everything like my father.

Eric does not say this, because he knows that it annoys me. He says that all three of us look very different except for the color of our hair.

Black is the absence of color, I reply.

I am most proud of my eyebrows. They arch the right way without needing to be plucked. Also, my mother has never pointed at them and demanded they change.

What my mother lacks in vision, she makes up for in hindsight.

Your nose: if only slightly higher. Your forehead: if only slightly wider. Your mouth: if only slightly more upturned, less sulky.

If only we could find the gene for beauty and bottle it.

The corners of my mouth naturally droop. I can't help this. But I try to combat it. I would say that at least 10 percent of my energy is dedicated to keeping my mouth in a straight line.

What Doctor Who said: A straight line may be the shortest distance between two points, but it is by no means the most interesting.

.   .   .

At the Arnold Arboretum, in fall, observe many people looking at trees.

Observe the dog misbehaving, gnawing on the leash so that he may run alongside bundled joggers and feel the breeze.

And Eric pulling back on the leash and clucking his tongue as he has seen a dog whisperer do on TV. But it's not whispering that you're doing, I tell him. It's just very loud clucking.

Observe no changes in the dog's behavior.

Eric is discussing us and has been for a while.

What are you afraid of? he asks.

Lots of things. The worst dreams I have are when I am falling. I am tipping back in a chair and suddenly I am going backward, toward a ground that does not exist. Falling feels like someone has taken my heart and dribbled with it.

I get no thrills from roller coasters.

Also spiders.

A few months ago, an egg sac hatches on our bedroom ceiling. I look up and see the ceiling move against little translucent dots with eight legs. Then the dots scatter. We stay up for hours killing them with toilet paper: him on tiptoes; me on a chair. We kill hundreds of baby spiders. We spray every surface with repellent and then sleep on the couch.

No, really, what are you so afraid of? he asks again.

I pluck a fiery leaf and put it in his hair. He is tall. Six one. And willowy. When iron oxidizes, it makes rust. But Eric doesn't like it when I call his hair color rust or even red. He prefers auburn. The first time he says *auburn* I mishear him and think he says *autumn*.

What am I so afraid of? Do I have to say it? You of all people should know. I have told you the most about them.

His argument is that they are not us and we are not them and their marriage is just one of many.

But genetically, it is very possible that I will be like both of them. And then that's bad news bears.

A jogger whisks by. When the leaf falls out of Eric's hair, the dog eats it.

I used to think this was funny, Eric says.

What's funny?

Us talking around in circles.

It was never supposed to be funny.

You're right.

. . .

There is a professor in my department who is no longer allowed to have graduate students. Under his tutelage, too many have committed suicide. He has unusually high work demands. He does this thing—asks students if they are busy and waits for them to cautiously say yes. Then he asks them to describe in detail what is keeping them busy for fourteen hours a day.

The students would begin to list off.

And also begin to sweat.

Bathroom breaks do not count. Eating does not count. If all fourteen hours cannot be accounted for, the professor deems a student not busy and gives him or her more work.

The last student to go has two roommates also in the apartment. He is considerate of them. On the bed where he dies, he writes, *Danger: Potassium cyanide. Please do not resuscitate.*

This is many years ago. Before I join the department.

How can something like that keep happening?

I have a guess. You get too wrapped up in your own work. You start to take lab personally.

Ninety percent of all experiments fail. This is a fact.

Every scientist has proven it. But you eventually start to wonder if this high rate of failure is also you. It can't be the chemicals' fault, you think. They have no souls.

One meaning of the word *tenure* is that if the lab as a whole does good work, as this professor had and won the Nobel for it, then certain things are overlooked. But after the potassium cyanide student, the school does make some changes. It adds a hotline for those who desperately need someone to talk to.

Just call and we'll listen, say the e-mails that are sent around.

But the line is always busy, say the colleagues who are downtrodden.

Is it?

I call just to see and get the busy tone.

. . .

My mother has a theory about hair. It is that the longer hair grows, the dumber a person becomes. She warns that too much hair will suck nutrients away from the head and leave it empty.

As such, my mother keeps her hair boyishly short.

As such, I am always pruning my split ends like a fiend.

After another day of no practical projects, I leave lab for the salon. I tell the man with scissors to cut off six inches immediately.

There is a scene in *Roman Holiday,* when the barber says, Off, off, and cuts off the princess's long hair. Then says, Now it's cool, hmm?

I worry that six inches is not enough. I ask the man to cut off two more.

Then I go back to lab and try again. Think small, I tell myself, think doable, think of something that might impress no one but will still let you graduate and find a job.

I gaze up at the ceiling lights, which are blinding, so I gaze down at the floor, which is dirty, so I take to folding a sheet of paper until I can't fold it anymore and then I fold another sheet.

You must love chemistry unconditionally.

But all I can think is how I am not up for the task.

Another theory about hair, not from my mother, but from the best friend. A woman who cuts her hair drastically is set to make some decisions.

Is eight inches drastic?

Finally, the lab coat comes off. I place it neatly into the drawer. Then I smash five beakers on the ground.

I shout, Beakers are cheap, while the whole lab gathers to watch.

I shout, If I really wanted to make a statement, I would have opened the argon box to air.

. . .

There is a prevailing hypothesis to why whales, in droves, will beach themselves on land. When the first whale becomes stranded, it sends out a distress call and then the other whales beach with it in solidarity.

There is solidarity in science to a point, but not when a coworker seems to be acting deranged.

Then it is best not to touch her or talk to her but to call the safety officer and watch the officer run down the hall with a fire extinguisher and a blanket.

Sound doesn't travel through space.

Sound requires a medium, tiny molecules vibrating.

Had I been shouting from a mountaintop where the air is thin, fewer people would have heard me.

I did not think I was shouting.

In my mind, I was whispering.

·   ·   ·

At home, I do mundane tasks like laundry and dishes and am amazed at how well they work. I add soap to a sponge and the sponge bubbles. I wipe the sponge on a dish and it cleans. I think, Sponge is better than catalyst.

I don't need to tell Eric what happened when he comes home. He is my emergency contact. The lab secretary has already called him.

He is kind enough to not ask any questions. Not even the most obvious one. Your hair, is it shorter?

He makes me oatmeal instead.

Am I a child? I ask.

No, he says as he feeds it to me on a spoon.

When we first meet in lab, he says that I have the steadiest hands. He has been watching me work.

Not in a creepy way, he adds. Then looks around nervously. Then leaves.

He finds me reading not a science journal but a book I borrowed from the library and gives me a thumbs-up. He used to read. He read up until he started grad school and then stopped. Where is the time? he says.

Books that he likes: *Heart of Darkness, The Stranger, The Trial.* Books that I like: none of the ones that he likes.

Is he cute? asks the best friend right away.

He's okay. Then I send her his lab picture and she replies, Oh my gosh, he is cute. Look at those eyes— light blue—and she calls them intense.

Soon we are working in adjacent fume hoods. This is the name for our chemical work space that vents toxic fumes into the atmosphere.

Can I borrow your sep funnel? Your hot plate? Your oil bath? Can I borrow your small magnetic stir- rer, if not your big magnetic stirrer, if not your paper clip, if not your . . . ?

When he runs out of things to borrow, he asks me out to lunch.

·   ·   ·

In 1986, my father moves to Shanghai. There are still thousands of bikes and thousands of bike bells. It is incredibly noisy, he finds. A year later, he meets my mother. Two years later, I am born. My mother, sick of changing and washing cloth diapers, teaches me how to use the bathroom at nine months. That's impossible, I am assured by everyone. How did you even get to the bathroom? My mother says I raised my hand and then she carried me.

But my father has no time for us. He has dreams of going abroad. To get into an engineering PhD program, he writes to every American university he can find. He writes to every professor in the field. He writes for three years.

His English is terrible. Please and sank you. And for what he cannot express in words, he uses equations.

Finally, a professor says, Come study under me.

I am five when we leave China and move to America.

In the beginning, my mother pays for everything. She does not like Detroit. It is a dirty, run-down motor city. Quarter mile to the nearest grocery store and you have to drive? She finds that inconceivable. She also doesn't know how to drive. She learns. But still it is nothing compared to Shanghai. In China, she makes more than my father, still a research assistant. She is a pharmacist, her mother an architect, her father a

physicist. She uses savings and her share of the family's money to pay for his tuition, our airfare, and the
first year of food and rent.

This is what my mother is referring to when she
says to him, You could not have gotten to this point
without me. Look at all that I have sacrificed. I have
given up proximity to friends and family. I have given
up my career. And for what?

For this: my father finishes his doctorate in record
time, three years, and then he gets a well-paying job.

His advisor tells him: You work the same amount
as twelve full-time graduate students. If only I had
twelve more like you.

But for this reason I do not see my father much.
I see my mother more. She is often in the bed-
room, hand wrapped around the phone cord, calling
China.

China is twelve hours ahead, she tells me. It is
always in the future.

When my father comes home, they fight in the
kitchen.

Enough, he says whenever she brings up the past.
Before overturning a table, he says that he too feels
underappreciated for all that he does.

He had done the work, hadn't he? He had gotten
a job. So he reminds her, What gives you the right
to judge me when you could not have done this and
when you do not even have a job?

The table goes over. A crash. A lull.

To be a pharmacist in America, my mother has to go back to school and retake all the tests.

She has a hard time passing those tests. For one, everything is written in English.

It is easier to do nothing about the table. Just stand up and wipe the debris off your legs. Then act as if you are about to leave the room, as she does, but before leaving the room completely, snap around to say one last thing. The more indifferent sounding, the better.

Break everything in this house, she says. See if I care.

. . .

At home, I do more mundane tasks like talk to the dog. I say, Heel, with the authority of a doctor. He heels and asks for nothing in return.

Why do you want nothing? I ask. You must want something.

A treat, a ball, I offer them to him, and he just wants to nuzzle.

We nuzzle, his wet nose on my dry one, and I forget, for a moment, the sound of five beakers hitting the ground.

Seven times a day, I walk him. It comes to a point that when we get to the park he just goes into the shade of a tree and lies down. He won't come when he is called. A flyer I see in this park offers free counseling to new parents. It is meant for parents of human children. It quotes a woman named Peggy: The way you talk to your human children becomes their inner voice.

Who is Peggy? I ask the other dog owners. And does she have a PhD to back up such claims?

There are other flyers posted, one that is seeking tutors in math or science. EXCELLENT PAY, it says, DOUGH, DOUGH, AND MORE DOUGH.

I take this flyer with me. I could use dough.

To buy the things that I want.

Like pizza.

. . .

Some people suffer externally. The dog, for instance, yelps in pain whenever we leave him alone in the house, even for one minute. His suffering takes him to the closet, where he hides and cowers until we come back, one minute later.

What must this feel like? The closet. So I go in there and wrap my arms around my knees. It feels as you would expect—epiphany-less and full of clothes.

During my first year in lab, someone who is graduating says, There comes a point in the doctorate where you just have to finish no matter what. If you don't, everyone will look at you differently.

I wait for that to happen.

But the bus driver who never looks at me—when I get on, get off; when I wave and say, Yoo-hoo, hello— is still the same.

I had imagined a sinkhole opening up beneath me

or at least a moderately sized fissure, but the ground is still the ground.

When I run out of things to do, I put in the same load of laundry I just washed.

· · ·

A week later, I call the number on the flyer.

How does this sound for a starting rate? says the woman, but I don't hear the actual number.

Was it three pizzas an hour?

I meet these students at the public library. I am allotted one hour per student to teach them whatever it is they have come to learn. Beforehand they fill out a request form.

First-year gen chem.

Second-year orgo.

Electricity . . . and magnetism . . . and circuits.

Usually I look at the form and say, I don't think I can do this in an hour. But maybe if you come back next week and the week after that and the week after that.

They are mostly college kids. But to me, they still seem very young. Wow, I say aloud when one of them has never heard of a floppy disk.

What was so floppy about it? she asks, and I say, You had to be there to know.

In general, I tell them to ask me anything. Ask me things you have always wanted to know.

How hard is invisibility to achieve?

Seriously?

Seriously.

Very hard. First, you must have transparent organs. Second, you must have the same index of refraction as air, that is, light must not know that you exist and go through you as it does through air, straight, unbending. Glass, for instance, is transparent, but light still bends when it goes through it, so glass is not invisible, unless you happen not to notice it there and hit it on your way out.

Regardless of what they have requested to learn, I ask each student to jot this down anyway: Light has five properties in total. It is not just one thing; it is a spectrum.

When I add that light, for being so multifaceted, is also really, really cool, they jot this down too.

Refraction is why I am not invisible. It is also why things in water, like fish, appear farther and bigger than you think, and once that fish gets pulled out of the water, you are vastly disappointed.

Lots of fish proverbs:

Big fish, small pond.

Small fish, big pond.

Looking for fish? Don't climb a tree.

Looking for fish? Go home and weave a net.

Gone fishing (with a net). Catch you later.

. . .

When we arrive in America, my mother starts teaching me about China. She thinks I will forget. She teaches me the four great beauties, the four great inventions, the four great novels.

She will ask me who was the first emperor of China and for how long did he reign?

The dynasties, list them.

Qin, Han, Sui, Tang, Song, Yuan, Ming, Qing.

Your memory is somewhat astounding, Eric says, but why can't you remember to shut the cabinets or turn off lights? Why do you so often put the bowl in the microwave and forget to hit start?

To the question that he is now posing from the kitchen—Who forgot to feed the dog?—I say, The dog.

During the early months of our dating, neither of us gets any work done in lab. We are perpetually flirting. Wear your nicest things, says the best friend, wear makeup, and I ignore her, because what is the point of nice things and makeup when you are in a lab coat and safety goggles all day? Though once, I try on a pair of stilettos. I can stand at my hood and run reactions. But I can't walk. I can't get back to my chair and sit down. Eventually I call him over for help. Maybe it was just an excuse to hold hands.

When he isn't looking, I leave small gifts on his desk. I do this stealthily or what I think is stealthily. I ask him what his favorite thing to eat is—a spicy burrito—what his favorite thing to drink is—bourbon—and then leave those things. I open his lab notebook and draw something on a distant page. He likes Pac-Man so I draw a lot of Pac-Mans. He likes Mario but I can't draw Mario very well—the mustache, difficult—so I draw another Pac-Man.

Soon he catches on. He comes to find me, a stern expression yet playful. Here is how you draw Mario, he says. But he too finds the mustache difficult and tries many times.

. . .

The lab mate is not there when I break the beakers, but she must have heard or noticed my empty desk. She calls a month later.

When I don't pick up, she leaves a message: Would I be interested in skydiving? Because if so, she could take me. She knows a place. She goes semiregularly.

Nothing will make you forget your troubles more, she says, than jumping out of a plane.

The message goes on.

If not skydiving, then bungee jumping.

If not bungee jumping, then zip-lining.

Do you like metal? she asks. What about moshing?

Finally, I pick the phone up. This is very nice of you but I don't think I can do any of those things.

Are you coming back? she asks.

I have to go.

What's wrong?

You won't believe this but there is a bear in my backyard.

Then I hang up.

Obviously, there is no bear. It is the dog, whom we have not groomed in months.

The lab mate is a good person but sometimes I think, had I never met her, I would have asked less often, Why would a field need me when it has someone like her?

A proverb my father made up: To progress in life, you must always compare yourself with someone better and never with someone worse.

These things happen, Eric says about my one-month absence from lab. The one month is a grace period. Then, swiftly, I am put on medical leave and in contact with a shrink.

.   .   .

I have procured a bottle of gin from the liquor store and placed it on the table. Now I am watching the liquid inside disappear.

Did you do this? Eric asks when he comes home and finds an empty bottle in the trash.

I'm sorry, I reply. I should have put it in the recycling. I know glass belongs in the recycling.

One thing that I am grateful for is the enzyme that breaks down ethanol. Without it my face would turn alarmingly red and no one would trust me with alcohol again.

Did you eat anything? he then asks, shedding both

coat and bag at the same time and gliding into the kitchen as if on Rollerblades. I think he is on Rollerblades and ask him to go back to the door and do that again.

When I am like this, I am highly susceptible to food commercials. Tyson's 100 percent all-natural ingredients fully cooked chicken nuggets. My face inches closer and closer to the screen and Eric must pull me away before I hit it.

Together we make another trip to the supermarket.

Not a trip, I correct myself, an expedition.

See me skip sidewalks altogether and dodge in and out of ferns.

.   .   .

I lose track of the days.

Is it the weekend? Or is it microwavable spring rolls day? Every meal, we eat off paper plates on our lap. No more dishes, I decide. Too much work.

End of fall weather:

There is an advisory out for hailstorms. I am out when it starts and little flecks of white stab my eyes. The hail comes down hard and fast and pelts everything. Then what follows is a freakish rainstorm where standing outside for a millisecond feels like being hit with a high-powered hose.

There is an advisory out for high winds. Gusts of more than forty miles an hour are expected. We close all of our windows and climb into bed. But we can still hear the sound of branches breaking and falling and trash cans lifting off.

This stupid city, I say the next morning, when I am walking through the street, looking for our trash can.

· · ·

Eric has something to tell me. He brings me to the couch to do it.

Are you listening? he says.

Listening.

Perhaps you should go see this shrink.

What shrink? I had tossed out the contact information immediately. I had not even entertained the thought of going.

Do you think something is wrong? I ask. Because nothing is wrong. I'm entirely happy.

My laugh that follows. It is very manic sounding.

· · ·

With my father, I do not like asking questions. He is not tall, but at ten, I must crane my neck to see him. For every question I ask—Why does ice float on water? Why are negative numbers not prime?—he says, You have a brain and two hands. You can look up the answers yourself. Then a question he poses to me: Did anyone teach him advanced math or did he learn it himself? Yet, ironically, he teaches me. But the kind of teacher he is: once he says something the first time he will not say it again. You have a brain and two hands, look up the answers yourself. You want to know how to get through life? Pay attention.

A habit that forms from this is that I can ask Eric questions only when he is asleep.

Once I hear the first snore, I say, Why is your trajectory so straight? Why is your family so nice? It seems unfair how easy everything comes to you. In your last life you must have been a dung beetle. Or someone who gave up his life for someone else. Perhaps a pregnant woman crossing the street.

Do you remember?

Then I part his autumn hair and bring my voice down to a whisper. Please stop, just for a little while, and let me catch up. How do you expect me to marry you if you never let me catch up?

I am braver now. I can say these things when he is awake.

Go talk to her, he says. This time very firm, very serious.

I mean it, he says, this time very quiet.

.   .   .

In those initial sessions, I arrive at her office in big sunglasses and a long puffy coat. Halfway through the hour, she says, Feel free to take off those sunglasses any time, and I make up some excuse of why I can't, my pupils were recently dilated. These are the only prescription glasses I have.

I sit as close to the door as possible.

I never take off that coat.

Also, it is the start of winter and I am perpetually cold.

Once home, I tell Eric that I had seen her, was he happy?

To the woman in charge of my health insurance, I ask, And you're sure that my parents will not find out about the shrink?

Not unless you decide to do something drastic, she says.

Like this? A dream I recently had where I was swimming in an Olympic-sized pool of dichloromethane, a solvent that burns when rubbed on skin. I swam and swam and drowned.

The woman says, Yes, like that.

I find it funny, just the thought of what my mother would say if she knew I was going to see a shrink. Talk to a stranger about your problems? Pay a stranger to listen?

. . .

The first time Eric says I love you, it is in lab, before a meeting. He thinks he will wait until after my meeting, but he has been anxious all day. He hasn't slept.

He catches me before I walk into the conference room
and just says it. I freeze. I feel my skin burn to a crisp.
Do I go to this meeting? I do but remember nothing.

What the shrink says from day one: The chasm you
need to cross is not a physical one.

Then what is it? I ask.

I much prefer the physical one. Tell me to walk
across the Grand Canyon on a tightrope, balancing an
apple on my head, and I'll do it.

A year into our dating, Eric says he wants to understand me and not just from a distance or through what
he calls my ten-inch-thick bulletproof glass.

Behind this glass, he says, he has found more glass.

An involuntary tic I have is that I cannot hold
hands for a long period of time. My thumb eventually
digs into the center of his palm and makes him let go.

Hold my hand like a normal person, he yells.

I'm sorry, I yell back.

He is baffled we are still having this problem. We
are out with the dog. We are out getting takeout. I
meander back and forth. He then grabs my hand
again and I focus with all my might to not move the
thumb.

· · ·

Here is a joke a classmate tells me in middle school:
When an Asian baby is born her parents hold up two
signs, DOCTOR or DOCTOR, and the baby must choose.

By now, I have heard many versions of this joke. Times change, so no longer DOCTOR or DOCTOR, but DOCTOR or SCIENTIST. DOCTOR or ENGINEER. DOCTOR or INVESTMENT BANKER.

It isn't so much of a joke as a statement.

Where did you hear that? I ask her, and she says her parents, who are white. Then I watch her bend over with laughter. When she bends back, I want to kick her. She asks if my parents ever held up signs. I say no. She says they must have. I say no. Then she goes up to the teacher and calls me a liar.

This classmate and I never become friends. I wish I had kicked her.

When I say this to the shrink, she says, Stand in front of a mirror. Your reflection is a way to deal with episodes of anger.

But I'm not angry.

Oh yes, you are.

· · ·

I am now tutoring more students. The ones who write down magnetism and electricity and circuits come to me because other tutors turn them away. Can you help? they ask. I will try. But it is not easy being teacher. How to stick to one topic for a set period of time. How to lesson plan.

The things that I say:

First things first, are you hungry? Do you like chips?

Pen only so that I can see all of your mistakes and, hopefully, correct them.

The chips are gone? They're gone? All right, you stay here. I will go get more.

During one session, a student who is trying to learn magnetism starts to tell me about where he grew up.

On an island.

In the middle of the Atlantic.

Where there is only one dentist.

Who is his father.

I know he is only trying to kill time, but it is a compelling enough story that I let him finish. Then I tell him another story about teeth.

Have you ever seen radium in person? It is one of those beautiful fluorescent chemicals. At the end of the twentieth century, it was being used to make glow-in-the-dark watches. To paint each watch, girls dipped their brushes in a pint of radium paint and then washed the paint off in their mouths.

What is not known then is that ingest enough radium and it will go straight into your bones. Radium like calcium. There is a reason that these two are in the same column of the periodic table.

The teeth of these girls were the first to decay.

And then everything else.

To completely rid a body of radium, you must cremate it and then boil it in hydrochloric acid.

After this story, the student is ready to get back to magnetism. He passes me the blank worksheet we were supposed to have finished in this time.

———

I read somewhere that a good teacher summarizes every lesson.

Don't drink the radium paint; drink water.

At least three liters a day.

I hand the worksheet back, completed.

. . .

We are home. It is raining. The whole apartment has a wet dog smell to it. This happens because we have given him free rein of the furniture. A couch. A bed. A coffee table. Two rugs that he rolls around on as if they were grass. How does he get wet in the first place? Eric takes him outside. When it rains, the dog is thrilled. He is a strange dog that likes to get wet.

Perhaps we don't do enough together, I suggest to Eric. We don't go anywhere anymore. Didn't we used to do more?

What do you want to do? he asks.

What do *you* want to do? I ask.

Later that week, the best friend says, Oh my god, he's not made of glass, you know.

Maybe not glass. But porcelain?

I don't remember ever seeing my parents hold hands, or hug, or kiss. I wonder if this is why when I hear affectionate words, I want to jump off tall buildings despite a crippling fear of heights.

The shrink says, It would be impossible if they never did those things because you're here.

What do you like about me? I ask Eric that night.

Huh? he says.

Then later when I smile he points to the smile and says that.

. . .

We decide on the Museum of Science. The museum has a planetarium and a Beatles laser light show.

The song list: "Dear Prudence." "She Said She Said." "You're Going to Lose That Girl." "Oh! Darling." "Everybody's Got Something to Hide Except Me and My Monkey." "Nowhere Man." "A Day in the Life."

But I don't like the Beatles, I say softly to Eric while we are standing in line for the show.

You know I don't like the Beatles, I say while we are settling down into our seats.

I like Queen and Freddie Mercury, the song "Don't Stop Me Now." The lyrics, just listen: *I'm a rocket ship on my way to Mars, on a collision course. I am a satellite, I'm out of control, I am a sex machine ready to reload, like an atom bomb about to explode . . . call me Mister Fahrenheit.*

Freddie Mercury made science cool, I say, knowing how cheesy that must sound.

Also, his name was Freddie *Mercury*.

Eric grew up listening to the Beatles. His mother is a Beatlemania survivor. His father, a reformed hippie.

Give them a chance, he says.

During the show, I get carried away by the lasers. There are so many of them.

A laser is colorful by emission. It is green because it emits green light. It is not like a leaf that is green because it absorbs red light.

Some students have trouble with this—whether the color they perceive is through emission or absorption. Then I tell the student, If you can see the color in the dark, it is its own thing, it is emission. In this way, a green laser is a purer form of color than the world's greenest leaf.

After the show, everywhere I look—a white wall, the blue sky, Eric's face—I see lasers in the shape of owls and submarines.

You didn't like it, he says.

I did. I like trying new things.

You don't.

I don't.

What about "Dear Prudence"? he asks.

Which one was that?

When I finally figure it out—the first one. The first one? The one with the owl laser. Which owl? The green owl. Ah, that one, that one was okay. Just okay? Pretty good—he has seen enough of the museum and now wants to leave.

———

Eric introduced me to music. Before him, I was listening to silence. And yet I played piano for ten years.

From age seven, I start to learn. I am classically trained. At the beginning, I practice three hours a day with Ping-Pong balls strapped to the palms of my hands. My fingers grow. I can span an octave. My favorite piece is the "Raindrop Prelude," but I can play "Für Elise" through without music. I don't because of stage fright and because the one time that I do, in a café, during high school, a man comes over and says, If I hear "Für Elise" again I think I will scream, it's so overrated. For a moment, I almost scream. I perform well enough to play for the choir and accompany singers but not well enough to carry my own concert. You don't have the emotion, my Russian piano teacher says. You play everything correctly, the pedaling precise, but you play like a robot, without pain or sorrow, without happiness or joy.

Eric is so musically inclined that at any moment, a song is playing through his head. Hence why he can often be found humming. He grows up forming bands with his friends. They call themselves names like the Derk or Aqua Hamster. At one point, he is in five bands, along with marching band at school. He is told that playing the drums will get him chicks. Actually the friend says it will get him laid. Not once does that happen. He does not get laid until college and not because of drums. The girl just finds him cute. There is a jazz band at this college and he signs up.

In jazz, they teach you how to improvise, he says,

so that you are not just playing the music on the page.

I don't know what to make of that. Not play the music on the page?

Last year, at Macy's, he stops to inform me that the song playing overhead is in five-four. We have not been talking about music; instead we are walking through and admiring the holiday decor. But the time signature, two measures in and he will know.

I tell him that he must have a gift and he shakes his head. Every musician can tell you that.

Not me.

There are musicians and then there are people who know how to play instruments.

What are you trying to say?

Not you specifically but people in general.

Still we fight beside clothing racks.

One thing he says: If you could be an emotion, it would be spite.

One thing I say: If you could be an animal, it would be a sloth.

But I only say that out of spite.

My ears must be broken. I know what "Dear Prudence" sounds like. I have heard it a dozen or so times. Eric has also played it for me on the stereo and said many things about it. The following day, he says, I was hoping you would have said something else besides good or okay.

I take a stab at what I should have said. Something about the beat perhaps.

Was it beat-y? Beat-ish? Beat-le-ful?

None of those, it seems, as he looks away without laughing.

.   .   .

Every day in December, the weatherman calls for snow. Finally, it snows. I don't know what I am more surprised by, the flakes or the weatherman being right, though he did stack his odds.

I get up early, at five a.m., to admire how white everything is, before the plow trucks come through and the dogs pee on all of it.

.   .   .

You need to know at least three thousand Chinese characters to read the newspaper and I might know a thousand. I cannot write any of them.

I have visited China only twice after leaving: once in the middle of junior high and once at the end of high school. When I go back the second time, I am given more freedom. I am allowed to go places by myself. This is nice I think until I get into a cab and ask the driver to take me to a restaurant where I am supposed to meet my mother and her friends. I can say the restaurant's name fluently, without an accent, but the driver doesn't know where the restaurant is.

He asks me to write it down so he can type it into the GPS. In the end, I have to get out of the cab and find another.

I don't find another cab. I just walk the twenty blocks or so, mortified.

A new fear I have is that I am losing my Chinese-ness. It is just flaking off me like dead skin.

And below that skin is my American-ness.

As a child, I often dreamed in Chinese, but I have not dreamed in Chinese for a long time. The steps in my logic, thus, ergo, hence, are now all in English. Oddly enough, I still count in Chinese, so I try my best to count everything that I pass.

Three bananas.

Seven bicycles.

Twelve babies strapped to twelve adults.

This way the skin stays intact.

It is a strange sensation to not be entirely at home in either language. I am more comfortable in English, but Eric says that he can still tell I am not a native speaker—Your idioms are always a little off and you say *close* for everything. Close the lights, the TV, the oven. You say *close* when you really mean *turn off*.

Because in Chinese, there is only one word for it. *Guan.*

Before Eric is there to correct me, I say things like *tone death* or *don't judge a book's cover* or *furried brows.*

Brows are furry, are they not?

They are, he says, but furriness is not a state of frustration.

After losing a game of anything, I will say, Don't rub my face.

You mean *Don't rub my face in it.*

Yes, that, but also don't rub my face.

Of the many Chinese dialects, I speak only one. My mother speaks an additional one.

With her family and friends in China, she speaks Shanghainese. The dialect sounds entirely different from Mandarin. It is more lyrical, more beautiful, considered by some (my mother) to be the most beautiful dialect of Chinese. The first time I hear French, I think of her. The blending of syllables is similar, the sung nature of it. After learning that the French have tremendous pride for their language, I understand a little more about her.

Although he lived eight years in Shanghai, my father cannot speak it. This might be because she does not speak it with him—they speak only in Mandarin. When I am born, she does not speak it with me.

Studies have shown that the brain feels exclusion not like a broken heart but like a broken bone. It is physical pain that the brain feels.

I know a little Shanghainese. It is impossible not to learn any. *La ta* means extremely unkempt. She says this when describing me, my room. *Dan di* means to call a taxi.

Why do you need to know everything that we are saying? she asks at the restaurant I finally get to, her childhood friends around her.

I guess I don't need to know; I would just like to.

I think of this later, that maybe she doesn't teach me because Shanghainese is hers just as English becomes mine. I am fluent by age six and it must annoy her. Even now, people still talk to her in loud voices, as if speaking English poorly is the same as being deaf. People still laugh, as if it is the same as being very funny.

Though at times it is a little funny. The summer before college, painters came to work on our house. My mother could never say the word *painters*. She says *panthers*. When the neighbors asked, she told them there were three panthers in the house.

.   .   .

Reflection is the easiest property of light to explain. The front side of a spoon is a concave mirror. The backside is a convex one. At dinner, I carve out extra time to admire this interesting fact. I pull the spoon toward and away from my face and stop at the moment my nose turns upside down.

What are you doing? Eric asks.

Spoon staring.

But why?

To rid myself of anger.

.   .   .

All comedies end in marriage. All tragedies end in death. But what about everything else in between?

Life happens in the middle, I heard someone very smart say.

I ask Eric about us. So what do you call this?

Limbo, he says.

A word that reminds me of a Latin dance.

What has changed while we are in this dance:

We no longer share the same blanket in bed; we have two separate blankets.

In a field, I throw a ball from one end and he throws it from another and the dog must choose.

The dog just sits there. This is a trap, he thinks.

TV watching is a struggle. He says, No more Food Network. Or Bravo. Or TLC.

Then what is there to watch?

The best friend says, Whatever happens, happens, but do no harm. Don't just break it off for the sake of it. Don't do something drastic just to prove a point.

She would rather it come down to the wire than have the patient throw in the towel too early.

Do you guys still cuddle? she asks.

Not at first. But then when I wake up we are, my legs over his, his arms over mine, the dog on top of all that. We must move into these positions when we sleep.

. . .

How do you explain color to a blind person? Not completely blind but almost. A task I have because one of my students is like this. She can see a glimmer of things but only if she looks long and hard. She can see that the sky is somewhat blue and that the sun is somewhat yellow.

Very good, I say. That's dispersion. That's when boring white light goes through a prism and comes out a rainbow. Blue light disperses the most, hence the blue sky you see everywhere. Yellow light disperses the least, hence the yellow sun you see in one place.

I am supposed to be helping her prepare for the GRE. Instead, we spend most of the time talking about color.

The color of my clothes and shoes.

The color of other people's clothes and shoes.

The color of the sky when the sun has dipped just low enough to cause red light to bend the most and then, voilà, a sunset.

In the middle of the periodic table are transition metals. These metals have weird properties and are colorful. Manganese is lavender. Copper is royal blue. Nickel is seafoam green. Cobalt is dark orange. And chromium has lots of colors, depending on what state it wants to be in. I tell her that I used to work with these metals in lab.

So don't ever say gray like metal.

Say gray like fog, like smoke, like ash.

She says, Gray like elephants?

I suppose that works too.

The next day, I get a call from this student's mother.

My daughter has said nothing about the GRE. All she ever talks about is color. Is color on the GREs?

No, it's not. But it should be.

What are you really teaching her?

How to make sense of sunsets.

After I say that, the line goes dead. On the day of our next session, no one shows up, and I come home to Eric talking to his mother on speakerphone. I hear him describe to her his day in detail, down to the condiments he used for lunch. Ketchup with cracked pepper. Mayonnaise with honey.

He says the job search is going well. He has many interviews lined up.

I'm not surprised, his mother says.

My sun and stars.

Brilliant, brilliant.

Some advice on happiness: the surest way to be happy is to seek happiness for others.

The shrink adds, And if you can't do that, then fake it.

. . .

Every so often, the school calls to see how my leave of absence is going.

It's going, I reply.

And your health?

That too.

To the students who tell me they want to be scientists, I say, Are you sure? Do you know?

Scientists are mere mortals and mere mortals make mistakes.

Theorems are only theorems because they have never been proven wrong, but they have also never been proven right.

It is all a great big loophole.

Then what am I actually learning? one student asks.

Correct. So do you really want to be a scientist?

There is no snow in January but there is this deadly freezing air. From the window it looks deceptively warm and sunny, but once outside you feel your skin cells start to die. I wrap myself in a blanket just to go get the mail.

The best friend has sent me a present. It is a stuffed doll with yellow yarn for hair and two Xs for eyes and a line for a mouth. It is called a Dammit Doll. I am to grasp this doll by the legs and whack the stuffing out of it, while shouting, Dammit, dammit, dammit. I try, but the doll has proven to be made from industrial-grade stuff. I have named it Science, You Motherfucker.

. . .

Before we started dating, Eric would walk by my hood and compliment my vials—how pretty they were. Pretty chemistry for a pretty girl. And I blushed. I didn't think I was that pretty. I wasn't as pretty as manganese.

Now he walks by my desk in the apartment and hands me the phone. He is one of those people—an optimist. He is encouraging me to call my parents and speak the truth.

But my parents and I rarely speak. And when we do, it is not to chat about condiments.

My mother asks: When are you finishing your doctorate? When are you getting a job?

My father asks: When are you paying back your student loans? When are you buying a house?

They both agree that I should stop being a child and start being an adult.

In college, I had a Chinese roommate who called her parents every Sunday.

In college, I had a Chinese roommate who cried for two hours every Sunday.

To prevent this from happening I lie.

They don't know that Eric and I are living together. I am terrified to tell them. I can't imagine telling them. Before Eric is even in the picture, my father asks that I do not move in with a guy until marriage and my mother asks that I do not change my last name. They say this sternly. I do not ever hear them use the word *sex* but it is assumed no sex until marriage. I think the Chinese phrase for it is *go to bed*. Or maybe *go up to bed*. I think but I don't know.

Married women in China keep their last names. My mother finds the Western tradition of changing it old-fashioned: Why bother with gender equality in the first place? For this reason, she has trouble understanding why people still think the Chinese are backward.

I have heard it too. Said by curious classmates, said by a man I sat next to on a plane—the Chinese, being both backward and upside down, a directionally challenged race.

What is repeated many times must then be true.

In China, rain comes up from the ground and lands in the sky. The moon and sun have switched places. Everyone reads from right to left and everyone is getting younger. Hence the belief that Asian women never age.

What's the worst that could happen? says everybody.

And when all this encouragement gets to my head and I finally work up the nerve to tell them: Mom, Dad, I'm not going to finish my PhD. I'm quitting.

My mother says, Don't call me again. Don't even think about coming home.

She says, Who do you think you are? You are nothing to me without that degree.

And then she says nothing because she is banging the phone on the counter.

It is a metaphor.

Eric looks on apprehensively. What's happening?

he asks, and when I put the phone banging on speaker he says, Oh, that, and promptly leaves.

At our next session, the shrink calls this metaphor psychological warfare. You must rise above it, she says. They're just words being said many miles away.

That phrase about sticks and stones and bones.

But my bones are very brittle. And I am lactose intolerant.

.   .   .

What J. K. Rowling said during a commencement speech: There is an expiry date on blaming your parents for steering you in the wrong direction; the moment you are old enough to take the wheel, responsibility lies with you.

I realize that I am no good at this wheel taking. There is fear and guilt.

I can't stand it when they are mad at me. I can't sleep, and once I can't sleep, I can't do much of anything else.

Five sleepless nights ensue, along with fear and guilt and persistent shaking and shivering and trying many times to tie my shoes but being unable to hold the laces and having to ask Eric for help, and wanting to throw up but also being unable to because I haven't actually eaten anything.

I run from every woman with short black hair and

every man of stocky build. At every turn, I think it is them coming to question me.

Accidentally I flip to a movie, some thriller where a young girl is being stuffed into the back of a car by a couple in black masks.

Her parents, I suspect. Who else would do such a thing? And once I reach that conclusion, I scream and throw the remote across the room.

It is a chicken-and-egg argument.

Did I go into science because I liked it? Or because I was, at the beginning, very good at it and then began to like it?

What Eric likes about chemistry is that the atom is the foundation for everything else. It is four years ago, at the scene of our first date, an International House of Pancakes, after lab, a late dinner or an early breakfast—it's three a.m., we realize.

To understand life at the molecular level. To understand the universe at the molecular level, he says.

An atom is mostly made up of empty space.

If you remove the empty space from every atom, the entire world's human population could fit inside a sugar cube.

Finally, I tell Eric that this is not sustainable, the persistent shaking, the remote throwing, the dog bringing the remote back each time and placing it squarely in my lap because he thinks I'm playing a game.

They will come around, Eric says.

How do you know?

Because they're people too.

Somewhere, there is probably a Chinese proverb about this—parents are parents, and to people who are not their children, they are people.

If I am ever to sleep again, I must call them back and lie.

You just caught me on a bad day. I will finish the PhD soon and then get a job.

Good is all my mother says before hanging up.

The power they have over you, Eric says. I just don't get it.

But you can't even tell me the worst thing your parents have said.

And that's a bad thing?

I often wonder what I would have been like if I had been raised like him—notes, stickers, complimentary questions asked at the table, by the hearth. I would probably socialize better in large groups and not stare so intently at shoes. I would hold my neck up high like a giraffe, the most confident of mammals.

. . .

A joke:

What do you do with a sick chemist? Helium.

Or curium.

Or barium.

.   .   .

Being in limbo doesn't preclude us from sharing nice meals. In limbo, we still have to eat.

February: a cold and dreary month but also when many nicer places have prix fixe menus to bring in poorer customers such as us. We go to an upscale Italian restaurant in Back Bay where the scenery is quintessential Boston—a row of lampposts, a row of brownstones, a crystal chandelier in every window. Is it brownstone or is it brickstone? To me, the latter one has always made more sense. At the restaurant, I can decipher some of the menu through deductive reasoning. Antipasto is not-pasta, like antimatter is not-matter.

Eric wants to know, if not now, then when. If he has a time line, then he can better plan for next time. If in a few months, then he will keep the ring box in the drawer. If in a few years, then he will put the ring box into storage and ask again, when I am ready.

I sometimes think Eric was destined to go into science. Edison tried ten thousand lightbulb filaments before he found the right one. Between Leonardo and the Wright brothers, it took five hundred years for man to fulfill his dream of flight.

After mentioning that I don't really know when, I list some girls with whom he might be happier.

Mutual friends. These girls are fun and vivacious and have the same interests he does, in music specifically. They are fine with just listening to music as an activity. They like the Beatles and progressive metal and bands I don't know. They could talk with him about polyrhythms. Polyrhythms are a thing, I think.

I look out the window at the falling snow.

I mention the happiest of our mutual friends, a girl who is prone to spontaneous acts like bounding through six feet of fresh snow to buy used books at the bookstore.

But I don't want a girl who bounds through six feet of fresh snow, he says, while swirling red pasta onto his spoon. I want a girl who stays inside.

That night, I lie with one cheek on his bare chest. I listen to heart sounds, the ones of valves opening and closing as blood goes from atrium to ventricle, ventricle to arteries, and back around. The circulatory system is a closed system, which means nothing goes in and nothing comes out.

The first rule of chem lab is to never heat a closed system or it will explode.

. . .

The most emotionally charged experiences, particularly those linked to fear, activate parts of the brain responsible for long-term memory. This makes sense evolutionarily, since being able to recall fearful events is critical to not dying in the wild.

One example is childbirth. Mothers are often amazingly accurate in recounting the duration and intensity of pain but are less so with the specific details of the child.

It takes my mother ten hours and twenty-three minutes to give birth.

I am induced.

No pain meds.

What did I look like? I ask, age seven.

Like a baby.

Anything else?

Like a potato.

The reverse must also work, that of the child recalling memories of the mother.

This is also what the shrink has asked me to do.

Once, she parks the car horizontally across the driveway such that for my father to leave, he has to drive across the lawn, through the rosebushes and then the mailbox. There is no mail that day.

Once, she cuts all the phone cords in the house. She is tired of calling places like Big Lots and Marshalls and asking if they can offer her a job. Over the phone, they can hear her accent and say that the job was recently filled. But after she cuts them, she regrets it. How can she call China now?

Once, she sits in bed for three days and three nights, drinking cooking wine, writing letters. I don't know to whom. I think the letters say something important. But I can't read them because they are written in Chinese.

In return, my father breaks every single plate in the house. Then he stands in the doorway of her bedroom yelling. Don't just sit there and feel sorry for yourself, he says, Get up. She gets up, gets angry, pushes him out the doorway so that he stumbles and falls. How she manages to do that is a feat. She is a petite bird and my father, a bulwark.

What else? the shrink asks.

Maybe this: I felt invincible when smashing those beakers. But then I felt worse. It was unkind to make the beakers suffer on my behalf.

Attributing feelings to inanimate things is probably a symptom of only-child-ness. Who else to talk to when the parents fight except walls and banisters and things?

. . .

It is now another meal on another day. Deductive reasoning breaks down in restaurants where everything is written in French.

So I must ask, What is an *aperitif*? What is an *amuse-bouche*? What is a *la carte de vins*?

This restaurant is very elegant, the tables made of marble. I envision my mother picking up the napkin with two fingers and spreading it across her lap. The image of the uncouth Chinese she first encounters in America. She doesn't understand why we are considered rude, considered dirty, until she walks into a Chinese buffet and walks out. In Shanghai, nothing is like this, she says. In Shanghai, the floors are clean. The waitstaff is nice. In Shanghai, you can get any kind of food you want. But what is sweet and sour pork? she asks, and is not pleased when she tastes it. In Shanghai, you can't get that.

Wine, Eric says. *Vin* means wine.

A cart of wine, I think, and ask the waiter to please bring the whole cart over, along with a big straw.

What happens if Oberlin gives me an offer? Eric says.

Is that what you really want? I say.

It might be ninety-nine percent of what I really want. It is the best school for what I want to do.

Then, I guess, I would keep the dog.

Would you consider coming? he asks.

In the mind of a scientist, beauty is simplicity. The most elegant experiment is the one that takes no time to set up and gives the answer to every question.

Yes, I had considered it.

In an ideal world, I would go with him without qualms. Ohio, I would say, how different. Let's have a new adventure there with the dog.

But once there, I would be plagued by other thoughts.

I am the girl who followed you and I know what

happens to those girls. They are never happy and then they carry that unhappiness everywhere.

Eric has said this many times before. The comparison you are making is not the same. Ohio is still part of America. They still speak English there. You will have less trouble making friends. And who knows, you might even like it more than the city, what with all that space and fresh air.

After we're home from the French restaurant, it is the start of another big fight.

Though big is also quiet, because when mad, Eric says nothing. He sits and stares off into space.

When really mad, he stands up and goes to another room.

I find that I am most like her in this way. I will follow him into that other room to say the same things I had said in the room before. Hello, are you listening? Hello, are you deaf? But that anti-temper of his is unassailable.

It's late, he finally tells me. Let's just try our best to go to sleep.

Then he turns the shower on for me. He hands me a freshly laundered towel. And I almost don't want to take it. A moment ago I had said, Let's just stop talking about it and break up. Yet the towel he gives me, he still drapes carefully around my neck.

· · ·

Studies have shown that dogs do not adjust well to new homes and will inevitably try to find their way back to their old one, even if it means running head-on into oncoming traffic.

But what about their owners?

Do they run into traffic after them?

When I show these studies to Eric, he says, This tells me nothing.

It tells you something.

Here I go again, out into the wind and snow to walk the dog, who is so worked up to get to the park and pee on a snowman. Then we see the toddler who runs across the tundra to hug the yellow snowman and the mother who runs swiftly behind to stop her.

. . .

Tonight I can't sleep. I think perhaps I would be more comfortable on the couch instead of the bed, but once on the couch, I realize the leather is very cold, the ceiling is very dark, and any second now, spiders could be crawling out from under the seat cushions and into my mouth.

On average, a person swallows eight spiders a year in her sleep.

Scientists have been trying to debunk that myth for years. They keep saying that we humans are too big, that to spiders we are just landscape and that our vibrations (breathing, snoring, beating of the heart) would send any spider crying for the hills before it got anywhere near the mouth.

But once I heard the number eight, I could never un-hear it.

Also, can spiders cry? I don't know.

At dawn, Eric carries me back to bed and I ask him what he thinks. He is groggy but sharp. He reminds me that spiders have exoskeletons and the point of exo-skeletons is to keep all the fluid in.

.   .   .

Come visit, come visit.

Okay.

By train I go, arrive, and wave to the best friend from a sea of other people. Here I am in bright yellow pants and a white sweater and a coat that is too thin. I have not visited her in a year. I have forgotten that all of Manhattan is a wind tunnel.

You look like a banana, she says when she sees me. It is a joke, but I am sensitive. Bananas are packed with nutrients, she says when I start to freak out.

The best friend is one of the lucky few. Her parents are similarly strict and push her into medicine. Begrudgingly she goes. In college, she studies biol-ogy and likes that lab mice do not talk back when she kills them. The idea of bedside manners. The idea of giving families bad news. But in medical school, she finds it not terrible. The other students are but not the patients; they are kind. The ones who are not kind, she doesn't fault because they are in extreme pain. After her first twenty-eight-hour shift in residency, she still has the energy to call me. She is hyped up on coffee. She keeps talking about pigeons. How do you know that you couldn't have done something else? I ask. She says, Honestly, I can't see myself doing anything else.

I have requested of the shrink: Find me the thing that I can make the greatest impact in and I will do that thing.

You and everybody else, she replied.

For a while, I have a running list of other viable occupations. Writer of tour group agendas. Taster of new and bizarre foods. Watcher of people from park benches.

We don't even make it out of Penn Station before I say to the best friend, about science, I think there is still magic in it but I couldn't find it.

Forget science. What about Eric? He might leave without you.

But what am I supposed to do?

Make him stay. Or go with him.

I can't.

Which one?

Either.

The best friend now sees that I have packed nothing for this visit. No water or change of clothes. No bags. I have just brought myself and the banana suit.

Never mind, she says. What can I do to help?

We go café hopping. SoHo. The Village. Skim cappuccino, please. We go bathroom hopping soon after. I find it bizarre that she knows where all the good hotel bathrooms are in the city but is clueless when it comes to subway stops. It is better to walk anyway, she says. That spiel about clogged arteries. The bathrooms, though, are exceptionally nice. There is one with glittery blue tiles. Another with cloth napkins and a lady butler.

I never thought sitting on a toilet could be so relaxing. It is a high-tech toilet from Japan. I press the button with a beaming sun and get mood lighting. I press the button with a musical note and get Mozart.

At last the news she's been waiting to tell me comes out.

Oh, baby, I say.

Due this summer. She rubs her belly, still flat, but growing a millimeter each day. Stretch marks terrify her, and then there's the actual work of raising a child.

How hard can it be? she says.

Not hard, I say. Just don't shake her too much, let her sleep, let her do what she wants, tell her the usual things like follow your dreams, and then remind her that sometimes these dreams must be let go to make way for more realistic ambitions like money to pay the bills.

The best friend wants her baby to be a model, if she has the legs for it, or an actress, someone beautiful and famous but not necessarily very smart.

I see where she is coming from.

. . .

When a woman gives birth, her body releases large amounts of oxytocin, a hormone that helps with maternal bonding.

This hormone has many other names.

The moral molecule.

The trust hormone.

The source of love and prosperity.

Not all mothers show the same peaks in oxytocin. Some show very, very high levels. These are the ones who refuse to let go of the child. Others show no peaks.

When I first learned that, I thought, Very possible. No peaks.

. . .

In parenting magazines, I look up what it means to be a good aunt and find nothing. I find instead an interview of a famous model who is now a mother. She says that she was first drawn to fashion after watching her own mother dress up in front of the mirror.

I read interviews of other models. A common sentiment, it seems, is this mother in front of the mirror, dazzling them.

The best friend must know. I call her but she is at work. So I page her and she calls me right back.

I tell her to go out this minute and purchase one full-length mirror, one long string of pearls, and one beautiful dress. When the baby comes out, she must dress in those every day in front of the baby and then change into scrubs at work. Your baby can never see you in scrubs, I say. Or the illusion will be lost and she will think you ordinary and herself ordinary and not want to go into modeling or fashion.

What are you talking about? she says. In the background I hear a siren.

I know association is not causation. I know causation is harder to prove, unless you have at your disposal a crystal ball or time machine that can go back in time and remove the mother from the mirror and see if the girl still becomes a model.

Or remove both parents from the mirror and see if the girl still pursues a PhD.

If I could go back in time, I would first win the lottery and second win the lottery.

If I won a million dollars, I would invest it.

You are missing the point of the question, Eric says. A minute ago, we were discussing my lottery winning scheme. But what would you do if you had that much money? he finally asks. I tell him. He replies, money is not the point here, it is what you choose to do with your time thereafter.

If he had a million dollars, he would play drums all day long.

If he had a million dollars, he would read.

See what I mean, he adds, and now I am annoyed.

Fine, I reply, if I had a million dollars I would go on a brief vacation and then invest it.

The Chinese so often seen as utilitarian. But truthfully isn't this what most people would do? Who would win a million dollars and just read? Also Eric has no time for drums. He stops playing them when he stops reading books. Where is the time? But more important, where is the space? The soundproofed walls? Where is the band? He tries to join a band at the beginning of grad school but then has to leave, because where is the time?

When I remind him of all this, he is annoyed. You take everything so literally.

On weekends, he is gone. He must fly out to each college for an interview and impress them with Power-Point slides. When he practices the presentation in front of me, I am impressed. What if you add lasers? is my one real suggestion.

The dog and I stay home. Hold down the fort, he tells us before leaving.

Aye, aye, Captain.

. . .

Jot this down as well:

To understand light is to understand its spectrum. It is a long spectrum but there is reason to it. Ultraviolet comes after violet and infrared comes before red. If you take everything back to first principles, you will never have to memorize anything again.

I then point out the window. See how the light outside is bluish, the shadows longer. That is because we are still in the dead of winter and the sun is in a lower position in the sky.

The dead of winter goes until March. I bundle up heavily and then go outside, but the stupid wind cuts right through the down feathers and layers of cotton shirts. I can't even frown. My face is frostbitten.

When it gets too cold to bike or walk to the library, Eric drives me. Then picks me up. Thank you, thank you, I say when I get into the moving heated box. Thank you, oil and pistons. Thank you, Henry Ford.

There is a period of time when my students wonder if I am angry at them.

What? No. Why would you think that? Because it's cold? Everyone is angry about the cold. Who doesn't want to punch a cloud these days.

Then I realize.

It's not that, it's because I lie on eye exams. I prefer less than sharp vision and therefore must squint all the time. This has made others think that I am giving them a look of disdain when I am only trying to make out their features.

So I try to remedy this by looking at each student with eyes wide open and eyebrows raised.

Now they ask if something they said surprised me.

I decide that it is better to look surprised all the time than to look angry.

The eye is a converging lens so named because it converges light, much like a magnifying glass.

Don't stare, my mother tells me when I am a child and looking around. I see a couple kissing on the bus. I see old people holding hands. I am fascinated by these public displays of affection because it feels like watching a crime. Don't stare? But why not? The eye is a magnifying glass. Growing up, I have perfect vision until high school. Then things start to get blurry. I like this blurriness. There are some things I would rather not see. Everyone has acne, but why does my acne seem to be the worst? Everyone has parents, but why do mine seem to be the worst? Also the looks from other people when we walk out in public, not because we are Chinese, but because sometime during the trip, we will start to argue.

Buy this, not that. Who pays for rent? Who pays for food? Just stop, the two of you. What did she just say? Did you hear her? Who does she think she is? Little princess. Little empress. Parents can't even talk anymore without the child chiming in.

I am never grounded, never sent to my room without a meal. My parents find these punishments too easy. They believe a child should be made to feel bad for her actions, so their idea of a scolding is to talk about her as if she is not there. The third person is used. The looking right past her. Whatever she says is not acknowledged, but once she mutters something back in English—This is bullshit.

Is it the English or the impertinence that sends my father over the edge? Immediately, the slap across the face.

.   .   .

During another weekend without Eric, I spend my spare time at a grocery store famously known for its free samples. The best friend finds this bizarre. Why are you always in a grocery store?

Because the aisles are neat and well stocked. Because everything, or almost everything, is edible. It is calming. You should try it. The best friend would rather not. She has weekly groceries delivered. Now, that, she says, is relaxing.

I am in line for a sample and then loop around to get another. I wear the same set of clothes for three days.

At the deli counter, a boy of ten is telling his mother, Satellites are constantly falling around the Earth. The mother thinks him absurd. Where did you get an idea like that?

I don't want to interject, but while waiting for the sample of smoked ham, I do anyway.

Actually, he's right, for the same reason baseballs fall after you throw them, satellites fall as well. But the curvature of the Earth prevents them from ever hitting the ground.

When I say, Think of how many home runs that would be if the baseball never touched the ground, the boy smiles but the mother, who has been eyeing me, pushes him along.

A meter is the distance between two marks on a platinum bar in Paris.

A meter is how much chocolate I have eaten since he has been gone.

One day, I end each tutoring lesson with this fallacy. A study has shown that European countries with higher chocolate consumption also produced more Nobel laureates. This would seem to suggest the path to a Nobel is paved with cacao beans. But how do you know that the people eating chocolate are the same ones winning the prizes?

You don't, I say, while breaking off a piece of chocolate and giving it to the student.

Diet starts tomorrow.

A weird problem I have is that fat collects only on my abdomen and never on my arms or legs or below the chin.

Lucky you, the best friend says, who is growing all over. She says the glow they talk about is a lie. Glow is just another way to say fat, sweaty, and radiating hormonal rage. She feels like a crazed hippo most of the time.

I think the glow is probably still there, just hard to see, in the ultraviolet or higher.

When Eric comes home, I let the dog rush to him instead. I won't tell him that I have eaten through two pounds of smoked ham.

Eric sees the number of wine bottles on the counter.
What's this? he asks.
A sale. Buy two get one free.
But why are they all empty?
It just happened. But look, now we have three new vases.

. . .

Before I can read names, I think every boy in America is named Ben and every girl is named Jen. My elementary school alone has seven and six of each. To reduce my confusion, I number them, Ben One, Ben Two, and Ben Three. Something I notice about this new culture: the common first names, yet the emphasis on being an individual.

My mother's American name is Joy. She picks it out herself.

During a free minute between tutoring, I stare at my phone and imagine myself calling her. I could tell her about the letter. The school has sent me a letter. It says that I am no longer a student there. They call it a permanent separation and then they wish me the best.

The goal of a science PhD is to have an original idea. Those who cannot are often called technicians. A technician is able to follow a protocol but not able to think beyond it. The best PhD students make the jump from technician to scientist in less than a few years. The worst never make that jump. Some advisors realize this early on and advise these students to leave science soon. Other advisors allow them to reach that point themselves.

When we are both in the same lab, I ask Eric, How did you do it? The jump. And he explains to me the flowchart in his head, how after each experiment, his mind directs him to another box that builds off the results of the last one.

Afterward, I begin waking up each day, hopeful that my flowchart has appeared and then crushed when it has not.

Eric is the first to tell me.

Not to say that you're not a good chemist, you are, but maybe this is just not your thing.

It is the first time I am this angry with him.

Not my thing? I shout. Who does chemistry think he is, God? If I want it to be my thing, it will be my thing. I will make it my thing.

Everyone is a genius, said Einstein. But he also said, A person who has not made his great contribution to science before the age of thirty will never do so.

Likewise, a mathematician peaks at the age of twenty-six. For whatever reason, after that young age, the creativity needed to do the work diminishes.

I show the school's letter to the shrink. See here the stamped signature. See here the serious font.

.   .   .

In addition to the Fortress of Solitude, there was another room for chemicals. It was a storage room but Eric thought up a different name, the Batcave.

This scene: It is after he has said he loves me and I don't know what to say. I don't say anything he wants to hear. We fight, cool off; we don't want to talk to each other for a few days and don't. In those few days, there is a lot of looking and looking away in lab. There is a lot of walking around each other as if the other person has the plague. There is also third-party involvement any time one person needs to say something imperative to the other, something like We are out of nitrogen, please put in an order of nitrogen. We are out of distilled dichloromethane, please distill more dichloromethane. Your reaction is about to spill over, it's spilling over.

This could go on forever, we think, because who could be better at being cold and facetious than two scientists, but what neither of us can stand is not knowing where the other person is, if not in the adjacent hood.

So when he is in the Batcave, I go in looking for him.

When I am in the Fortress of Solitude, he comes in looking for me.

What? we say to each other, annoyed but feigning annoyance.

Eventually, I hand him a spicy burrito. On the foil wrapper, I have written out what he wants me to say.

. . .

A new student brings me a plate of cheese and crackers. It is our first day. He sneaks the plate into the library under his jacket. I am supposed to teach him something, but upon seeing the gift, I forget. What was it that I wanted to say?

I remember: Math is not something that you can learn in one hour. You have forgotten too much. I asked you what is the third root of sixty-four and you didn't know. You will not be ready for this test in time. You will fail, most likely, or close to it.

But instead of replying he pushes the plate toward me and asks me to take a bite.

The last thing I ate was a candy bar, yesterday. I am opposed to bribery in principle, but when it happens, I can still eat the food. The cheese tastes expensive.

I once had a math teacher who made me play a game. The teacher is my father and the game involves a deck of cards. He puts four cards on the table, number cards only, and I am to use any order of operation to get to twenty-four. I am to say things like two times two is four minus one is three times eight is twenty-four or ten times ten is a hundred divided by five is twenty plus four is twenty-four. We play this game whenever I have someplace else to be—a school dance, a party. He likes to say, For every second that you are not learning, you are wasting. He sees no value in a school dance.

The rule is I cannot go anywhere until I have beaten him, and he knows I can't beat him.

In general, a phrase I cannot say to him is *it's complicated,* even though this is what middle school kids are saying at the time. What homework are you doing? he asks, and I accidentally say that phrase. Nothing is ever so complicated that I can't explain it and he can't understand it.

What's so complicated about your life? he asks. You have no fiscal responsibilities, no taxes, no mortgage, no nine-to-five job, no job whatsoever except to learn and be a student.

Do not boast, he says, that your life is complicated.

Do not boast, period.

When I get into the best college in America, he is cutting radishes for dinner. I have just found out ten minutes ago. I am elated. He puts down the knife to shake my hand and then goes back to cutting radishes.

. . .

Some students have said that I do not give enough positive encouragement. They wait until the end of the lesson to tell me, and then they say it timidly.

Do you think I am doing better? I don't always know if you think I am doing better.

So I have practiced some phrases. *Almost, but not quite. Nice try. Way to go. Don't be so hard on yourself.* These words sound foreign to me, but I am now a roulette wheel of positivity.

When he gets a problem wrong, I tell the math student, Almost, but not quite. I say, Nice try, because he does try but the answer is still very far from his reach.

What is a rate? he asks.

It is a number divided by time.

What is a ratio? he asks.

It is a number divided by another number.

What is the difference between a rate and a ratio?

One is a subset of the other, like a square is always a rectangle but a rectangle is not always a square.

What is a square? What is a rectangle?

Don't be so hard on yourself.

At the end of our sessions, he offers me the cheese and crackers. Then he offers to drive me home.

Outside the snow is melting in large waves. Soon the streets will flood. But the weather is just being a tease. Tomorrow it will get cold again and then on and off like that until summer.

He is older than most college students I have taught, having traveled the world after high school for many years. Places like Patagonia, Tibet, Morocco, Vietnam.

Why on earth would you want to go to Vietnam? And suddenly I sound a lot like my mother.

I let him drive me home. Look here, I point to the number on his speedometer. This is a rate.

. . .

Lots of people stay together long-term and never marry, says the best friend. Finally, she has a weekend off work and spends it looking up famously unmarried couples for me. George Sand and Frédéric Chopin. Katharine Hepburn and Spencer Tracy. Why don't you two do that? she says. It doesn't have to be so all or nothing.

I take this to Eric.

And, Eric, think of all those men who love their mistresses to pieces but never end up marrying them.

He looks at me dumbfounded.

There are other things that bother him now.

At Whole Foods, I come across a handheld scanner at an empty register. I pick it up and point it around, whispering, *Pew, pew, pew, pew.* Eric takes the scanner away.

That was uncalled for, I say. I wasn't even *pew*-ing at you.

When we're walking the dog, he says that it feels like he is walking me too. You walk too slow and must see everything.

Who is going to do this when I'm gone? he asks while closing a cabinet behind me.

It is not as kindhearted in tone as before. It is more abrupt. And vertigo inducing. He has started to say things that he knows and I know but we have never really said aloud.

Isn't it obvious why you're like this? You didn't have a real childhood, so now you are lashing out.

But at night, there is still cuddling.

What do we think about that? I ask the best friend.

What do we think? We think that you are both out of your minds confused.

.   .   .

The official song of Ohio is a rock song called "Hang On Sloopy." I listen to it and find it catchy. But what kind of name is Sloopy?

In the center of the state is a field of eight-foot-tall cement corns.

In another part of the state is the world's biggest basket.

And somewhere, I read, there is a museum for all things swallowed that have been retrieved by the swallowers' doctors.

What I like about Boston is its closeness to the sea, but momentarily, I can see myself calling that strange state home.

I pose a hypothetical to Eric. If I go with you, will you take that other question off the table?

Until when?

Until forever?

He doesn't think so.

.   .   .

What the shrink says about hobbies: You should find some. Do you have any? You should find some.

What the lab mate says about hobbies: You can never do science as a hobby. Once you give up science, you give it up completely.

What my father says about hobbies: Growing a seasonal vegetable garden is essential.

I decide to follow an online fitness guru. It can't hurt, I think. Until it does, a lot.

She has this move called the burpee, which is a jumping jack that goes into a push-up that goes into a plank that goes into another jumping jack. I do just one of these and collapse on the floor.

Then I watch her do the rest for fifty more minutes. But this guru is great at pep talk.

The body achieves what the mind believes.

Sweat is fat crying.

You're a diamond, darling, they can't break you.

After every video, she reminds us that abs are made in the gym but revealed in the kitchen. I then go into the kitchen and pull up my shirt. They must be in there somewhere.

The shrink looks over my new hobbies. No to ab finding. No to vase making. No to— What is this? She squints to read my writing. Does this say seek out the homeless and provide them with lemonade?

Let me explain. There is this homeless man who digs through my recycling for cans. I know when he comes and offer him a beverage. If I don't have lemonade, it will at least be a cold glass of beer.

You give him beer?

Just one glass. Then I give him the can to exchange.

That's not a hobby. None of these are hobbies.

They could be. They're my hobbies.

Some people garden.

Plants hate me.

Or travel.

Where would I go?

Or photograph things.

What things?

Anything you want.

I don't know what I want. Isn't that why I'm here?

Commit to something, she says.

But what about the people outside of people?

Meaning what?

Every second, 4.3 babies are born.

The shrink excuses herself to get water. I see her shadow return but linger a few seconds outside the door. Eric has said that I carry close to my chest a ball of barbed wire that I sometimes throw at other people.

When I ride the train home, I miss my stop and must ride the train back. I calculate that in the time I have been in commute, fifteen thousand babies were born.

·   ·   ·

Our upstairs neighbors have gone on their honeymoon. They married a week ago on a beautiful spring day that initially showed signs of rain. And then it rained.

We call them Mr. and Mrs. Stomp in addition to their real names. She is a tiny girl with small feet and he is a burly man with monster ones. We can't figure out how they have sex comfortably, or look each other in the eye.

They have left their mail with us and gone to Santorini.

I have seen pictures of Santorini and don't believe that it actually looks the way it does. No place is really that beautiful. It is just a tourist trap. Once they arrive, I imagine a scenic cardboard cutout greeting them, behind which is a landfill of feta cheese.

It could be that beautiful, Eric says. How do you know it isn't? You haven't been there.

I'm extrapolating.

What arrives in the mail for the Stomps are packages. A box that says VACUUM CLEANER, FRAGILE. Another box that says VACUUM CLEANER, FRAGILE. A third box. It becomes quite comical actually; we didn't know about their vacuum cleaner fetish. Maybe this is how they have sex.

We pile all of these gifts outside their door. After a while, we can no longer see the door. In the same week, we discover that their apartment is leaking water into ours. A small brown stain appears on our kitchen ceiling and grows into a continent.

Does that look like Australia? I ask Eric, who says nothing, is very solemn. We can't confront the neighbors about this, because they are still living the island life. But in their haste to leave, they must have left their kitchen faucet on.

I find that hard to believe. Wouldn't they have heard it, so loud, the sound of a running faucet begging to be shut off? Think of all the fish they are killing.

But you do things like this all the time, Eric says.

No, never. I have never left a faucet on. I would have cried afterward, thinking of all the fish I had killed.

We tell the landlord about the continent.

Is it a very big leak? he asks.

Yes, huge.

Okay, I'll find someone to fix it.

But our landlord is neither punctual nor hardworking. And for many days, no one comes to fix it.

Maybe the Stomps mistook the sound of a running faucet for the one in their heads of them jumping from jagged cliffs into the Mediterranean Sea. Or maybe they did it on purpose, as a parting gift for us. If so, then they are terrible people, I say to Eric, and we should rename them the Shits.

Don't swear so much, Eric says. He finds this trait of mine unappealing, so unladylike.

There is swearing, I say, and then there is saying *shit*.

. . .

A running faucet is how I explain fluid dynamics to students. Put your hand here and feel it being drawn into the current. Moving fluids create low pressure, a vacuum, and suck everything around them in. See how thin the stream gets at the bottom, how skinny it is compared with the top? This is air pushing the water in.

A fluid by definition is any substance that has no fixed shape. Gas is a fluid, air is a fluid, which is why airplane wings are curved the way that they are. The top part allows air to move faster, creating low pressure and the lift that you call flight.

I wait for the aha moment that never comes.

Students also don't say *aha* anymore.

Eric goes to work. Eric comes back from work. What did I do in between? Laundry? No, the pile is still there. At night, before bed, he still lets me lean into his arm. But there are some nights when he leans into mine. Work is still tiring and then there is the added stress of waiting for schools to give him a job.

Drowsily, he says to me, Why are you doing this?

Doing what?

This. Us. Kangaroos.

He is in that almost asleep state.

. . .

The ceiling caves in and thirty pounds of moldy insulation come with it. Our food is buried underneath, our water, our alcohol—all the things that could help us get through this crisis are taken from us. The kitchen smells like a cave, sulfurous and damp, Pompeiian.

Should we call 911? I ask Eric, who is staring up at the hole in shock. I am holding back the dog. He thinks the wet insulation is rain and wants to roll around in it. But this I cannot allow.

In the end, we decide that it is not a 911 type of problem and call the landlord.

On a scale of one to ten, he asks, how bad is it? Eric takes the phone from my hand and starts shouting.

We go to stay at a dog-friendly inn for free. A village is hired to fix our ceiling. One week tops, we are told.

The inn has things like doilies on other things like tea tables.

At breakfast, Eric fills my coffee mug and then refills it when I shake my empty mug at him. Like a homeless person, he says.

But we *are* homeless. Get it?

The mark of a poor comedian is not making the other person laugh. The mark of a worse comedian is asking if the other person got it.

Then him to lab and me to tutor, while the dog stays in the inn with fresh water and food. These amenities are not enough, it seems. He scratches up the bottom half of every door.

I scold him when I return but am secretly pleased that he has left the same kind of markings on every door. In science, perfect reproducibility is the highest form of praise.

———

The village turns out to be an incredibly slow and ill-run village.

After one week, we are told, Another week, tops. Give or take a week.

.   .   .

It could be worse, you know, I tell the best friend, and she says, Really? How so?

The optimist sees the glass half full. The pessimist sees the glass half empty. The chemist sees the glass completely full, half in liquid state and half in gaseous, both of which are probably poisonous.

At the start of grad school, the safety officer warns us that working in a chemistry lab can shave five years off your life. Some things will never leave your lungs, he says. Silica, for instance.

Oh, well. Who needs to live that long anyway?

Because the inn has no kitchen, we have been eating a lot of granola bars.

I don't understand when I read on food packages that something is chemical-free. I immediately take offense. Everything is made up of chemicals. To say that something is chemical-free is to say that inside this package is an absolute vacuum.

Why would I pay this much for a vacuum?

Also, how much granola is too much?

The only difference between a poison and a cure is dosage. Drink too much water and you will die. Inhale water and you will die as well.

. . .

In the inn with the doilies, we are not always ourselves. One night, Eric leans over in bed and says, I want you. His voice cracks a little. He gets on top and the dog jumps on the bed and licks him from behind. We laugh about it, how rusty we are. To make things easier, we escort the dog into the bathroom and ask him to wait.

It comes back to me hurriedly. What Eric likes about "Dear Prudence."

The way it builds, throughout the song.

The guitar part is really pretty, and the bass part.

Paul McCartney killed it on the bass.

Pretty unconventional.

Pretty baller.

An intangible emotional reaction from the start.

And the beat, very simple at first but then surprisingly wild at the end.

Afterward, I let him play me the entire *White Album* with the lights off.

. . .

Chemists, long ago, used to stir their reactions by hand. I am being quite literal. They used to check for doneness with one finger in the pot. The mark of a good chemist used to be the number of fingers you had—the fewer, the better. It showed more experience in the lab.

Eric has all ten fingers and all ten toes. I joke that he must not be a very good chemist and he gives me a genuine laugh. But then the job offers come in. Including Oberlin, Ohio. He puts a doily on my head and dances me around the room.

The moment we're back in our old apartment, he asks the first question again. Say yes.

I want to.

He asks the second question. Come with me.

I want to.

Then say yes.

Isn't it enough that I want to?

. . .

I am twelve and unhappy. I am perpetually unhappy that year because for eight months, my mother hides knives under my father's pillow and I must put them back.

Often she pushes a blank piece of paper toward him asking for a divorce. He crumples the paper and throws it at her head.

Sitting in the backseat, I am terrified when he floors

it to 110. We are on our way to a barbecue. We are on the highway. The argument beforehand:

You are a fool. You are a crazy person. You think you got here all by yourself? Who pays the bills, the rent? Who bought this car?

A decade-long argument.

Soon, my mother unclips her seat belt and tells me to do the same.

We're getting out, she says. You heard your father. He doesn't need us anymore. He pays for everything now.

When I don't say anything, she begins to count.

I think I know what resentment sounds like. It sounds like my mother clicking the car door handle while counting to three.

But how did that make you feel, asks the shrink, and how do you feel about it now?

In times of extreme, extreme fear, the brain is awash in adrenaline and does not feel anything except for the fear. Then the fight-or-flight response kicks in. But where could I have gone? Stepping out of a moving car will first snap the neck. Then the body is pulled under the wheels.

How I feel about it now is the same as I did then. Not great. Pretty awful.

Studies have shown that in times of intense duress humans can develop superhuman strength and lift cars.

I report no such abilities.

Before she finishes counting, my father slows down. A police car is chasing us.

. . .

Eric has never jogged until now. I think it is to minimize his time at home with me. Outside, it is warm and joggers are rampant along the river. But Eric is the only one doing it in jeans and waterproof boots.

Would you rather spend eternity exploring the oceans or space? A question I ask after he has a bad day in lab. He comes home exhausted. He slumps into his chair. He sighs when I ask him anything, so I come up with silly questions to get him to talk.

He says space, because it is far away from planet Earth.

I say ocean, because at least it is still planet Earth. And think of all the sea animals. We could track down Nessie or Moby-Dick and then get rich.

Also, I remind him, being in space probably feels a lot like being in lab. For miles and miles, there is no one. The atmosphere is completely sterile.

But then I add, If you went into space, I would too. Space, the final frontier, I say in my best Spock voice.

. . .

I have been expecting this moment, haven't I? And yet why is the wind still knocked out of me?

He has said, just now, Some time apart wouldn't be the worst.

Perhaps I had never thought he would say it so casually, so word for word, and in the produce department of a grocery store.

Was that a question? I ask him.

But he refuses to look me in the eye.

He turns.

He throws a dozen apples in a bag.

Deer arrows are engineered to not go cleanly through, but to penetrate a few inches and lodge. Initially the deer does not feel excessive pain. Then the razor-sharp edges slice through the surrounding tissue as the deer runs. This causes hemorrhaging and the deer eventually bleeds out.

A quote: Reality is merely an illusion, albeit a very persistent one.

. . .

I did. I did say that I would follow him to space and that offer stills stands. But I did not say Ohio.

Fear of following the other person despite that person being good and reasonable and kind? What phobia is that? Stupidity?

. . .

Before he leaves the city, he wants to go to a jazz club.

Which one?

Ryles.

But that's just two blocks away.

He says he likes it anyway.

We walk toward a glowing neon sign. He is in a gray blazer that is slim fit and I am in a black dress that is too tight. All the eating, drinking. But I tell myself, Weight is just an artifact of gravity. If this were a jazz club on the moon, I would weigh less.

On this date, there is no kissing or hand holding or mentioning that this is a date. He calls it an expedition to tease me. He wonders why we haven't come to Ryles before.

Probably because it's just two blocks away.

I know nothing about jazz except Louis Armstrong.

That is a start, he says. Now what instrument did he play?

I guess trumpet and am rewarded with a smile.

We sit on plush velvet chairs. I see a bass, a trumpet, a drum set, a group dressed in all black swaying in the center of the room. I sit up straight, my back a plank of wood. If I don't focus, I will instead fall asleep, like I have many times at the symphony and woken up to find that I have missed everything. The applause for the encore. The encore.

Right now it is "What a Wonderful World." And next it will be "Caravan," but soon the band plays something that has no name and goes on for a long time. The crowd is drawn up to their feet and so is Eric. But what are they playing? What is this song? I applaud but think sooner or later someone is going to fumble.

Miles Davis: Do not fear the mistakes, there are none.

Louis Armstrong: Man, if you gotta ask, you'll never know.

Later that evening, Eric shares a neat fact with me. He has had a few drinks. He brings his face closer to mine. The neat fact: drummers will bury new cymbals to speed up the aging process that gives the metal an earthy sound. A *tah* instead of a *ping*.

I giggle when he says the word *earthy*.

Your puns, I say.

What puns? he says.

. . .

The breaking of bonds requires energy. This is a fundamental law of thermodynamics.

We walk along the river, arms crossed (me), hands in pocket (him).

The river is very polluted, I say.

Take care of yourself, he says.

College kids jump in there all the time.

It's three meals a day, and the occasional glass of wine.

One in ten succeed. The other nine swim to shore terrified.

Did you hear what I said?

Yes. Three meals a day taken with wine.

. . .

Packing commences. If he is to start in the fall, he must leave in early summer to set up his lab. The dog is frantic but strategic. He sits on shoes so Eric won't pack them. He sits on clothes so Eric won't fold them. He sits inside luggage bags so Eric won't close them. I try to lure him away with treats—big juicy marrow-bones, beef jerky, two scoops of vanilla ice cream—but he doesn't come.

Packing takes days.

We clean up the spot where he pees. He pees over Eric's ties. We take these ties to the dry cleaners and wait for them to call us. We clean up the spot where he poos. He poos all over Eric's best suit. We take this suit to the dry cleaner and wait for them to call us.

What's wrong with your dog? they ask.

Willful incontinence.

We finish packing when the dog has run out of ideas.

But not quite.

At the gate, he goes through his repertoire of tricks—

sit, lie down, crawl, play dead, roll over, high-five, sit, lie down, crawl, play dead, roll over, high-five. I ask him to please be dignified about this, but I have not yet taught him that command.

Dog, Eric says, and bends down to scratch his ears. Man, dog says, and lets out a long howl. Furried brows, both of them.

. . .

A frustrated dog will shed and now I must follow him around with a lint roller.

It's doable, I say to the shrink, to drive to Oberlin in one furious night.

But that is not love, she says, that is fear of facing your own demons.

I don't have demons, I say. I have students and a dog, but at night I do close all my closets out of fear of what might be inside. Dark matter, I believe.

I tell the best friend, He left and I let him. He said he would try not to call.

What are you going to do? she asks.

Not dwell. Move forward.

What are you really going to do?

Stare at spoons.

I tell the math student, Me and the dog make two, and two points define a line.

Remember what Doctor Who said about lines. Not at all interesting.

You need three or more points to define a shape.

The triangle is the strongest of all the shapes. When you think geometry, think triangles. The theorem that everyone knows by name, Pythagoras, is a theorem about a triangle.

If I could go back in time, I would design apartments that could not echo. I would revoke sound's ability to echo in the first place.

It is the echo and the dark matter that keep me up at night.

If I could go back in time, I would sleep and sleep.

But Hawking makes a very simple case for why time travel is not possible: no one in the past has come forward and no one in the future has come back.

. . .

There was a mnemonic I used to use in chemistry to remember the order of the four fundamental alkanes.

It was Me Eat Peanut Butter, which stood for methane, ethane, propane, butane.

I feel like I should not just be eating this stuff out of the jar.

. . .

The first time he asks, we are at the esplanade in the morning for a fireworks show that will start at night. It is the Fourth of July. We have brought a blanket, a basket, a dog. He has brought a ring, but I don't know that yet.

We wait for the sun to go down and the sky to light up. My head is on his lap the whole time.

And then the sky lights up.

I should have noticed the change in his demeanor. He is not cheering like I am but studying the sky. He is searching for the largest firework under which he will present me with the ring, not in the palm of his hand but, as he tells me later, like a telescope in front of my eye.

Not this one.

Or this one.

Or this one.

The largest one is coming at the end.

And then the barge from which the fireworks launched catches on fire and the show abruptly stops.

This cannot be happening, he says.

So we stay another minute while everyone around us scatters. When the barge is fully consumed by flames and other boats are speeding to its rescue, we have to be evacuated in case the barge explodes.

I say we'll come back next year, and he says he can't wait until then. I say we'll watch another show on TV, and he says he can't do that either.

I don't understand until on the train back, in a tunnel, he puts the ring on my knee.

PART II

A Chinese proverb says that the mastery of three things will make you fearless anywhere in the world. They are math, physics, and chemistry.

I have a few smart but lazy summer school students who want to learn all three as quickly as possible. They want what's in my head in theirs and wish that I could deliver knowledge more efficiently, through a tube, ideally, uploaded online.

Quality over quantity, they say, when they refuse to do the work that I have assigned.

So for these students, I have come up with a new assignment. Please sleep with your head on your textbook, and if you can recite the whole textbook by tomorrow, then I will concede to your genius.

Of course they try.

To be fearless means what? I ask the shrink. Does

it mean to be without fear or to have courage that is equal to or greater than fear?

The courage one, she says.

And where do I find courage?

At the library, when girls walk past me tutoring the math student, they slow down. They drop things like books and pencils and it gets too distracting, so we move to the café, where the same type of girl appears, dropping cups of coffee, and then stands in line again while glancing at him.

Had I noticed this before? His eye color is ivy. His hair color is sand. He is tall but not that willowy. I guess I can see the appeal. He often comes in wearing cool sunglasses and funky nautical-themed shorts.

But he pays no heed to these girls.

Why not? I ask. They seem so accommodating.

I then learn about the girl he feels strongly about, who feels the same way about him, but has said that it would never work out.

She can't possibly know that, I say.

But she's right, he says.

I then learn that the girl who feels the same way about him also studies extreme climate geology and spends most of the year in Antarctica.

I ask him to repeat that.

I had not heard that one before.

. . .

Many scientists believe that science cannot advance without sacrifices along the way.

Eric believes this. My father believes this.

Both have said something along this line of reasoning: the first man could not have known what was poison until he ate it and a second man was there to watch.

I try to picture this. How morbid. Did he really watch or did he run back to the village, arms flailing?

The math student meets the girl in college. They are on and off. He wants to travel the world first. But after he is finished, she wants to go to Antarctica. To get from here to that frozen place requires a mighty plane or boat. No car could get you there in one piece.

A southern continent was hypothesized to exist as early as the first century, but the South Pole was not reached until 1911. First by a team of Norwegians. A month later by a team of Brits. The Brits were disheartened to find that they were not the first to reach the pole. But even more disheartening was how, on the way back, the tin solders on their kerosene canisters broke and fuel leaked all over their food supply.

One member took ill and died.

Another went insane and wandered off.

The last three pushed on . . .

... then died, eleven miles outside of the British base.

I tell this story to the best friend.

What do you mean they all died? I thought you were trying to tell me a happy story.

No, I never said it was happy. Currently disaster stories are my jam.

Did you know that the same thing happened to Napoleon's army? Their tin buttons couldn't stand the Siberian cold and broke. All the men soon died from frostbite.

The best friend finds none of this interesting. Instead she tells me to leave the house at once.

If you don't, I will come and drag you out myself.

You can't. You're big bellied.

I'll send someone.

. . .

What is this feeling? The small pain under my rib cage. A deep soreness, which is impossible, because the heart cannot feel sore, because cardiac tissue cannot feel tired. To feel these things requires nerves that conduct sensation and the heart does not have such nerves.

But paranoid, I consult an online medical reference.

What could make the heart feel sore?

Heart disease.

What else?

Cancer.

But what could explain this feeling, that wherever you go and see a guy with slouched shoulders and red hair, you want to walk close behind him and see where he goes, not to bother him or anything, but just out of curiosity? Like yesterday, at the grocery store, down food aisles and freezers we went, him filling his cart with salt and coffee and baby food, me filling my cart with salt and coffee and baby food. Then I followed him out of the store. I watched him load the groceries into his car. Can I help you? he asked, and I ran the other way.

Cancer, definitely cancer. Maybe brain cancer.

I come away from this exercise believing in the good of human doctors. At least they give you options.

. . .

Who folds the laundry now?
No one.
Who cooks dinner?
The microwave.

. . .

In the middle of summer, my father calls.

There is no Hello, how are you? There is How is the PhD? How close are you to being done? You have not talked about the PhD in a while. I just don't understand why it's taking you so long to finish, you work too slowly, this must also be what your advisor thinks.

I will try to work harder.

Don't say *try*.

Sorry.

Don't say *sorry*.

I will work harder.

And don't say it for me. Say it for yourself. Have some self-discipline.

Okay.

After this talk, I go back to watching TV. I have started to watch competitive cooking shows. They are fun to watch because they are mindless. I notice that the Chinese American chef is always the one to say, I am here to make my parents proud. I want to prove to them that I can cook and that I am serious about it. More times than not the Chinese American chef will win.

When he loses he is the only one to say, Hopefully this does not make me a failure in life.

.   .   .

I ask the shrink, Why do they still encourage girls to go into science? I see flyers and commercials everywhere, and whenever I see them, I must divert my gaze.

Perhaps the fine print should read, If you are a girl with three balls, then please, please go into science, the field will definitely need you. Otherwise pick something else.

Chemistry has long been called an all-boys club, and yes, I agree this needs to change, but how to do it?

The great thing about science is that you are discovering truths about the world.

The bad thing about science is that you might not be the one to discover them.

Luck plays a huge role, but what Pasteur said about luck: Fortune favors the prepared mind.

Before I leave lab, there is another girl. She is very nice and high-spirited for the first year of her PhD. Then one day, I see her in front of the microwave, slamming the door and cursing it to hell. The advisor has given her an ultimatum: Either you give me results or I will fire you. To reach this deadline, she is soon found fabricating data.

She is suspended from lab indefinitely and every science PhD program in the country. A casualty of war, we call her. That of the mind against itself.

Sometimes it feels that I have failed many people. My father, for instance. The Chinese proverb about being fearless, he says it all the time. Could he ever see his daughter doing anything else besides math or chemistry or physics? If you ask him, he will certainly say no.

Engineers pride themselves on understanding how the world works. Imagine the core of the Earth as a heat engine, imagine the moon a perfect sphere. And I don't disagree; I like knowing how the world works too.

So why did I leave science again? I ask the shrink. Was it because I didn't like it or I wasn't good enough to do it?

Does it matter? she says. It wasn't your thing. Accept that and move on.

.   .   .

The dog and I are at a beach. I wake up this morning to clear skies, low humidity, and a sudden desire to see water. We then take the train to a place called Wonderland.

The trick to getting a dog to swim is to throw something he loves far into the water and then watch the anxiety get to him. He likes getting wet but not going into open water. Fear of sharks, most likely. He paces the sandy shore. He whines. Eventually he leaps into the water and becomes buoyant. The chew toy is saved.

Then I throw it again.

The time Eric and I go to a beach, I cannot sit still. I cannot lie down. I have not yet broken those beakers but I am thinking about it. While thinking, I write in the sand a list of things I'm not doing in lab because I'm at the beach.

Recrystallize X
Purify Y
Retry recrystallization
Retry purification
Start over

The integrated circuit was invented by a man who was still in lab during the week he was supposed to be on vacation.

I say to Eric afterward, Beaches make me nervous. I don't think I can go to one again.

Eric then throws a little sand in my face. Everything makes you nervous, he says.

But this time it is not so bad. The wet dog always comes back to me. It seems the chew toy is lost forever when he brings back a wad of seaweed.

. . .

Scientists like to say to other scientists, It depends on what question you are asking.

The question I am asking is: How to have fun without feeling like I am causing myself pain?

The best friend suggests weed. She's read that some of the best artists and musicians attribute their first experiences of joy to being high. Though not always on weed. Most often on amphetamines, but in good conscience as a doctor, she cannot recommend that.

Where do you find the weed? I ask.

No, it's just weed.

Weed. I say it over and over again. But it sounds so strange. I keep wanting to put in the article. Or if I say *weed,* I want to say *weeds.* Mister drug dealer, do you have any weeds for me today?

Never mind, she says. Just stick to alcohol.

. . .

There is another reason doing fun things causes me a tremendous amount of stress.

I am ten, eleven, twelve. I am trying to get through middle school but it is a rough time. I am made fun of relentlessly, the only Asian in school, minus another Asian kid but he is adopted and sticks to that line of reasoning—I am not like her, that freak. I am adopted and therefore terrible at math.

An aside that I am now coming to as an adult: When did being dumb become a virtue? He gets straight Ds to prove to his friends that he is definitely not anything like me, the girl who does the extra credit even when she has an A, the girl who likes to read textbooks and take notes.

On occasion, my mother picks me up early from this terrible school and I am profoundly grateful. She tells the teacher I have a doctor's appointment. It is believable; I am small for my age, bony. In the car, she tells me that we are going someplace fun.

We drive to Deer Acres Fun Park in Pinconning with rides like antique bumper cars and a merry-go-round.

We drive to Crossroads Village in Flint with rides like a steam locomotive and paddle wheel boating.

My mother follows me from one fun thing to another. She watches me do the fun things but never joins. She buys me popcorn but never eats it. Sometimes a smile, but is that a smile I remember or her wincing from the sun?

Then she drives us home.

Deadpan, a word I learned later on in high school, a casual and monotone voice that expresses a calm demeanor, despite the ridiculousness of the situation. A voice that an unhappy mother and wife might use with a child.

She asks if that was fun and I nod. She pulls into our driveway and tells me to get out.

What do you mean get out? the shrink asks.

I mean she would put the car in reverse afterward and leave.

What do you mean leave?

I mean go to a motel.

And then?

And then come back a week later.

. . .

The year I quit piano two things happen.

One: In the middle of a performance, my hands begin to sweat and I lose grip of the keys. I can't do the crossover or the trill or the doublet of triplets or even turn the page. And then I am stuck on the same page, the third of Sonata no. 5 in G Major, repeating from the repeat bar until the performance is over.

Two: The B-flat key doesn't play. I press it and press it and no sound comes out. The key is broken. Then I raise my hand in front of an audience of five hundred and say, May I stop now?

Some performers call stage fright *going up,* as in *going up into a mental vacuum.*

But it feels more like coming down and hitting pavement.

My parents do not come to my recitals.

Sure, my piano teacher says. You can stop now. And I never see her again.

It might be true that I was raising my hand at nine months. It has become so instinctual to always still be polite. Like now, at this bar, where I have raised my hand a dozen times to ask a question. Can I have another drink? Another drink? Another? When the drinks start to talk back (be careful with me, I am filled with hard liquor and dark thoughts), I tell the bartender and he tells me to leave.

The path of a drunk toward a lamppost is a classic model for probability. With equal probability, she will take a step left or right or forward or back. Such walk patterns have been used to model the length of a gambling game, the motion of a dust particle, the diffusion of neutrons in a reactor, and many other things.

I call Eric while en route to this lamppost. He answers. He answers so quickly. But when he realizes that I am not in grave danger, he says that he has to run.

Run where? You're already in Ohio.

He replies, Let's keep these calls sporadic but feel free to e-mail any time.

I try not to sound pitiful saying this: Can you stay on the line a little longer? I try but I fail. You don't need to say anything. Actually, don't say anything. Just listen to me walk home and I will listen to you walk home and once home we can both hang up.

But he has already hung up.

Later, the best friend finds me unbelievable. You called him and didn't tell him to come back?

I just forgot.

Even if I had made it to a wedding day, I could not have made it down that aisle. All those eyes on me, two per person. A joke Eric then made was that he would walk the aisle and I would stand up there.

But I could not have done that either.

There is no such thing as a perfectly still molecule. Even in solids, the molecules keep moving.

. . .

One more.

She drives us to Bay County Fair, my first real amusement park, with terrifying rides like the Sand Storm and the Zipper.

Outside the Zipper, there is a sign that says NOT

FOR THE WEAK-HEARTED, and then below that sign is another sign—WE MEAN IT, DO NOT RIDE IF YOU HAVE HEART PROBLEMS. I am just above the minimal height to get on. Like all foolish children, I believe my heart to be strong.

It is two and a half minutes of extreme spinning, with me in a free-moving cage that rotates nonstop. I am dizzy, light-headed, my vision so blurred that I cannot see anything except a smear of flashing lights.

That too is how I feel when waiting in the driveway for my father. Once he sees me, he frowns. Once we are inside, he throws things.

At you? the shrink asks.

At the wall, the TV. One time he tries to lift the TV but reconsiders: a TV is expensive, also a terrible shame to break the cathode ray tube inside.

I believed my heart to be strong, but not that strong.

. . .

The baby is born? The baby is born. The baby is born!

She is placed in my arms when the best friend visits on the first not so summery afternoon.

So tiny, I say. But what a disproportionally large head.

I touch the head carefully. I point: Here is your temporal lobe that controls speech. Here is your frontal lobe that controls thoughts. Here is your hippocampus that controls memory. All brand-new and humming.

The baby has black hair and black eyes and white skin. She looks charcoal-drawn.

Your brain must be tired, I say to the baby, who finally falls asleep.

What do I do now? I say to the best friend, who is also about to fall asleep.

Let me just lie here for a minute, she mumbles, and drifts slowly toward the ground.

The dog sniffs the baby and deems her okay. I decide to take them both out. Look, I say, there is the sun, the grass, the fresh air—all this you will take for granted someday and then rediscover with a baby in your arms.

How old? a woman asks from across the street.

I am not exactly sure. But I think 2.4 months and a few hours.

We go to three parks. We walk nonstop or else she cries. The baby likes moving, especially moving at high speeds, so we go on swings. She opens one eye and looks at me with profound suspicion. What is this contraption? she asks silently, a tiny cyclops in my hands.

This is a simple harmonic oscillator, I say, a pendulum; this is periodic motion.

Wheeeee is the sound I think her temporal lobe wants to make.

My new hobby is to teach this baby about the world. I will write it all down. Or whisper it into her ears.

I still want her to be a supermodel but, if possible, a genius one.

When we return, the best friend is awake but yawns after every sentence.

The husband has recently been promoted. He has more deadlines and late nights than before. How are they going to do this? In shifts, they decide. He sleeps while she mothers. She sleeps while he fathers. But to keep up with work, the husband must also be highly efficient. She says that at night, he makes business calls to Asia while rocking the baby to sleep.

Does she sleep well?

Not really.

I remember learning this at some point and thinking it was cool. While still in the womb, a baby is an aquatic animal. For the forty weeks before birth, it lives and sleeps in a water-filled sac.

What if you put on wave sounds? Maybe this mimics the inside of a womb.

The best friend says she hasn't tried. We try it, googling *ocean sounds,* but the baby couldn't care less about the ocean or waves. She likes the glow of the computer, the sound of any one of us typing.

Before they leave, I flap my arms around so that she will bob her head in that funny way.

.   .   .

I come back to C. S. Lewis's advice:

Love anything and your heart will be wrung and

possibly broken. If you want to make sure of keeping it intact you must give it to no one. Not even an animal. Wrap it carefully round with hobbies and little luxuries, avoid all entanglements. Lock it up safe in the casket or coffin of your selfishness. But in that casket, safe, dark, motionless, airless, it will change. It will not be broken; it will become unbreakable, impenetrable, irredeemable.

I do not want any of these things for my heart.

So, leave the casket and go elsewhere.

. . .

Leaf peeping is what it's called.

Every September, Eric and I drive up to New Hampshire to see the foliage. Then we find a bed-and-breakfast and do both of those things. Then we find the tallest mountain and hike it.

This year I go without telling anyone. I hike up the second-tallest mountain, while the dog blazes ahead.

Eric said to each passing tree, You have been peeped, and I said, Peep peep, coming through. The trees that were still lush and green we called *la résistance*.

This year, *la résistance* is in full swing. It has been a warm summer and now a warm fall. The dog is the first to summit while I am still a half mile behind, but he barks at regular intervals to guide me.

The second-tallest mountain has a better view, I realize, than the tallest one. There is a lake in the distance I hadn't noticed before.

At higher attitudes, the body makes more red blood cells to compensate for the thinner air. This is what gives athletes who do elevation training the competitive edge and also some hikers the feeling of being more alive.

Up here, I feel awake but no more alive. The dog on the other hand is running around in circles.

On one of our trips, Eric and I get lost. We have been following marked trees but then the markings disappear and the sun goes down fast.

Watch us panic. The forest smells of wet leaves and mildew. I can no longer see the details of his face or the dog's, but I can hear them both panting beside me. We hike one way and then another.

Which way is north? Eric keeps asking, a rhetorical question.

I look to the sky. I can find Orion's belt every time. But never the Big or Small Dipper. Never the North Star. The light from a star travels many years to get to us. What we are seeing is what the star looked like in the past. The star could be gone for all we know.

Finally, we come upon a river. We see beyond that river is a highway with cars. Cross, we say, and the dog does. Cross, we say, and stay exactly where we are. The dog is already on the other side when we finally wade into the freezing river with all of our equipment. The waters come to my waist. Rocks are slipperier than they look.

A year later, he says, I thought you were going to dump me that day.

Dump you? Why?

For making you walk through a river.

I didn't mind.

I know. That's when I knew we were going to work out.

. . .

Instead of a bed-and-breakfast, I find a motel. Why eat breakfast alone? I decide. Why give others more reason to talk?

The trouble with Chinese is that there are so many homonyms. Easily you could mix up the word for *mother* with the one for *horse*. The word for *mother* with the verb for *scold*. And then the two-character homonyms. The ones that I said when I was little and she would start to laugh.

You just said *coffee cup* instead of *comforter. Ice coffin* instead of *motel.*

But some motel rooms turn out to be ice coffins. Like this one. The heater is broken, the blankets thin. At night, the temperature drops below 50.

How did she do it? I wonder. Come to a place like this and stay for seven days straight. Did she eat? Or did she just sleep through it?

Bears give birth in hibernation. I imagine that to suddenly wake up a mother must feel bizarre, but there are no instances of the mother bear leaving her cubs from shock. It is possible that my mother had moments of shock when raising me. How did I get here? What am I doing? A daughter, you say? You must be mistaken.

When I first tell Eric about the amusement parks, he says, Your mother is a terrible person. Who does that to a child?

And then I put my hands up and say, No, no, no, she's not terrible. I explain my theory of shock. It shocked her sometimes to realize that I was there. And, I think, this prompted her to leave.

But that's no excuse, he says.

I have a hard time getting through to Eric what I think.

If my mother had done that to me, he says, I would have hated her for a long time.

The shrink also asks if I resent her and, logically, I think I should. What if someone had come along and snatched me? Also, didn't she ever want to leave my father a note, in case she decided not to come back?

If one parent should go, let it be the father. The absent father is more common and not always a terrible person.

Before Eric knows about all this, he takes me to Six Flags. It is supposed to be a surprise. I have just published that paper. What better way to celebrate, he thinks, than to do something he loved doing as a kid, in hopes that I will love it too. The rides: Wicked Cyclone, The Great Chase, Mind Eraser. But as we are driving up to the gates and I realize where we're going, I ask him to pull the car over so I can throw up.

He thinks I am kidding. He doesn't pull over.

Then, quietly, I throw up into my hands, and this makes him panic, drive faster, while I try not to spill the liquid in my hands.

. . .

I return from the ice coffin to find that the city has also cooled. The neighbors are not happy about it. Now there is only talk of how short this fall will be and then the long, impending doom.

During my time away, the best friend has made me an online dating profile.

Don't even think of it as dating, she says. Think of it as reentering the world and meeting guys along the way who can also keep you company while you eat.

Everyone has to eat, she says, and I don't disagree.

Also, she has called my body type svelte and my eye color umber. Because who has brown eyes these days? she says.

The questions she gives me to answer:

Describe your typical Friday night:
    Stay in, watch a movie, have debates with myself.

Describe your perfect weekend morning:
    Wake up, time stops, resolve debates with myself.

———

Look into my eyes, I am later caught saying to a receptionist at the DMV. They're umber or bister or taupe, but they are definitely not brown.

The debates that I have:

Popcorn, no popcorn, popcorn, no popcorn. Popcorn.

I'm fine, you're sad, I'm fine, you're confused and hurt and messed up and definitely not fine.

I once thought I would have all the answers by now.

Message me if . . . and I write, Message me if you know how rockets fly.

My gas particle trajectory problem might come from a simpler issue. In English, I cannot intuitively tell left from right. I can in Chinese, but in English, I must make my fingers into the letter *L* and the hand that says *L* correctly instead of backward is left. Eric found this funny. It was another way he could tell that I was not a native speaker. He would ask me to get him a mug. On purpose he would say the mug on the left, just so he could watch me make *L*s at the open cabinet to figure out which he meant.

The next one will not know of this small handicap.

I will simply never heed his directions and grab the closest mug I see.

The answers that I get:
Rockets fly in space because there is no gravity.
They can and believe that they can, and anything you believe in will happen with more or less certainty.
Fuel, duh.

I can count on two fingers the number of boyfriends I've had. How do I do this again? What do I say? The best friend says, Start with your name. Then ask him lots of questions, then use his answers to launch into more questions, then redirect any questions he has for you back on to him. Don't look sad.
But how do you know if he's interested?
If he shows up.
But how do you know if he's flirting?
If he shows up.

There is a guy with an impeccable sense of style who is better dressed than I am. At dinner, when I sneeze, he unfurls from his coat pocket a handkerchief with his initials embroidered on it. I pass on the handkerchief. I don't want to sneeze on anyone's initials.
There is a guy who gets to the point right away and

asks if I too am looking for something casual. If not, then forget it.

There is a guy who will not talk about movies. Movies kill the soul, he says. But films . . .

I tell him I know very little about films. Anything made before I was, I do not watch. Anything sci-fi related, he does not watch.

But what about *Gattaca*? I say.

I don't even know what that means, he says.

I do this sometimes: hold my breath for entire conversations with men and then feel faint. I cannot hold my breath past four minutes. At four, I must interrupt the guy who is talking and make a gagging sound.

Afterward there is no more talk of second dates.

What I like about *Gattaca* is that it is not what you think when you think of sci-fi. There are very few special effects. There is a man in lab doing work day in and day out. He waits for the centrifuge to be done. He pipettes something into vials. The movie is set in the far future and yet nothing about the science is flashy. The movie is timeless in this way.

.   .   .

Even in limbo, Eric still practiced Chinese. He was learning it for himself, he said, but when I told the best friend this, she said, Oh come on, he is learning it for you.

But I acted oblivious to this fact. What would it mean if he actually became fluent one day? Chinese is one of the hardest languages to learn, if not the hardest. It would mean that he cared for me a great deal. It would mean that I was crazy for not marrying him.

Before bed every night, he studies from a language app on his phone.

You don't need to do that now, I say.

It helps me sleep, he says.

I don't tell him that it helps me sleep too, him muttering Chinese beside me.

In the four years, he learns a lot of words. He can say simple phrases—*the sun is here; the moon is there; look, a door!* But whenever we visit my parents, he refuses to speak Chinese.

For an entire weekend, two years ago, he speaks only English to them and they speak only English back. I am beyond irritated. The looks of discomfort, especially from my mother. She forgets the word for *salt* and has to point to it. What that thing? she asks. Salt. Pepper. Pot. Pan. Eric doesn't notice her tone and tells her each time. Later, we whisper-fight in my old bedroom.

That was not your place. This is their house. Also, what good is learning all that Chinese if you are never going to use it when it counts?

We argue around this question. Does it matter? What's the big deal? The big deal? *The big deal?* I find myself no longer whisper-fighting. Eventually he says he just couldn't bring himself to do it. In Chinese, he couldn't get his personality across, or his humor. He felt limited.

Who cares about your humor? How do you think my mother feels right now, trying to get to know you?

That is not my problem. If she lives here, she is expected to speak the language.

The moment I hear him say that, I reach for the nearest heavy thing. A stapler. Perhaps I was planning to staple his lips together so that he could feel even more limited.

.   .   .

The leaf-shoveling business is tedious.

So I have hired the boy next door to do it.

But the overnight wind is wicked and blows every leaf in the world to my doorstep.

A fortune cookie says, With your walkways obstructed, you will have no more visitors.

My father's seasonal garden is doing well. It has been a banner year for eggplants. He writes me a one-paragraph e-mail to tell me and I spend the afternoon trying to read it.

The way Chinese is supposed to be read is in groups of characters at a time but I can't do this. I read one character at a time, with my finger glued to the screen. The words I don't know, every third, I look up.

Soon, he will harvest everything and give some away to friends.

Soon, I receive a package of three dozen eggplants.

This makes me think of the time he had me take back to Boston a winter melon. It was too big to fit into my suitcase so I had to carry it through security. When the officer looked at it with suspect, I had to put it through the X-ray.

The phrase *green thumb* he learns in America. But it seems strange to him at first. As a boy, he works long hours in the field. The machine he is using catches on a branch and stalls. He must put his hand into the blades and pull the branch out. He is a second too slow. Green thumb? he thinks. More like no thumb.

The three dozen eggplants arrive, meticulously packaged, with each eggplant wrapped in foil. I line them up from smallest to largest. I worry that eating this many will turn me purple.

Is that possible? I ask the best friend, who says, Hmm. Then she says that human biology is very weird, but if I do turn purple, be sure to let her know. It would certainly make her day.

Her days are very long. There is feeding the baby, then playing with the baby, then feeding the baby, then putting the baby to sleep.

And you would think it ends there, she says.

But no, she must also watch the baby sleep and see

the way her eyelids flutter during what we think is a very good dream.

The two of them visit monthly.

And I happily bundle the baby up and take her to the swings.

But when we come back, the best friend is often standing over a pot of boiling water, with her face in the steam. She read somewhere that steam extracts toxins and impure thoughts, like letting your baby cry herself to sleep or putting your baby into a box. She corrects herself: not a box, but something that will meet all of her needs up until she is eighteen and ready to go to college.

She says to be a good mother and wife is to be a perpetual motion machine.

The husband she last saw two days ago. A business trip, she thinks. Chicago? He had told her exactly where at some point but now she forgets. They are constantly missing each other's calls.

She says the steam is what's making her face red and puffy. Ignore the obvious other factor.

She says it is a phase that will eventually pass.

.   .   .

A list of famous chemists:

Alfred Nobel
Fritz Haber
Victor Grignard

The man who founds the Nobel Prizes is also the same man who invents dynamite, is called the Merchant of Death. Seeking to leave a different legacy, he gives his fortune to start the prizes, including the peace prize. This strategy works, it seems. I tell students about the dynamite and they are surprised.

Fritz invents a revolutionary process—a way to make ammonia from nitrogen and hydrogen. It is easy, scalable. Ammonia goes into fertilizer and the process is said to make bread available from air. But Fritz is also a complex person. Being hailed the father of modern agriculture is not enough. He goes on to pioneer chemical warfare, things like chlorine gas.

When I first see a picture of Victor, a French mathematician turned organic chemist, it is his mustache that I will remember—a massive handlebar that grows down from the nose over the mouth and outward, beyond both cheeks. He has a reaction named after him that every orgo student must know. During World War I, while Fritz, a German, is inventing chlorine gas, Victor works for the French to create phosgene, another gas but far deadlier and that smells of freshly cut grass.

Victor wins the 1912 Nobel for chemistry. Fritz, the 1918.

.   .   .

Recall that in science, perfect reproducibility is the highest form of praise.

When writing Chinese, the sequence of strokes is incredibly important. My mother tries to teach me— Draw the line first and then the dots, not the other way around—but quickly throws her hands up in frustration. Yet this systematic approach produces consistently beautiful handwriting. My mother's. My father's. I go back to China and realize that everyone writes this way.

How is it that I can always tell a Chinese person's handwriting by the way that they write their 5s? An elegant *S* with a long nose.

For many years, my parents send me to weekly Chinese school where I am to learn how to read and write. I pay very little attention. I talk all through class.

What do I need Chinese for?

An ancient language. A difficult one.

Yet that was my chance to learn more than I know and I wasted it.

If she lives here, she is expected to speak the language, Eric says.

Immediately, he apologizes. Immediately, I put the stapler down. But I can't forgive him. That thing you said, I have heard from other people as well. So I don't need to hear it from you.

Who am I really trying to forgive? That thing he says I have also thought as well. I have probably even said it. Her poor English is not for a lack of trying. She goes to ESL. She goes to reading groups. She is frustrated—a former pharmacist with a great memory but that memory is no longer there. Yet how this must have felt: in high school, I walk ten feet in front of her whenever we are out in public. She asks for help and I pretend not to hear her. Then when she tells the neighbor there are three panthers in the house, I am mortified. I correct her. Only later do I see humor in it.

Ching chang chong, sing me a song. Boys on the playground, taunting me. I skip Chinese school that week.

Ching chang chong, all night long. Boys in the classroom, taunting me. I skip Chinese school that month.

. . .

Who did you play with when you were little?

Do you have cousins your own age?

I don't feel like answering those questions, so the shrink asks an easier one: What did you do today?

I watched the dog chase himself around a tree. He thought his tail belonged to another dog. This is an improvement, no? It's like the more evolved form of tail chasing.

The shrink says she doesn't know.

Outside, it is freezing. It is a pain to breathe. The weather people predict that this winter will be the coldest one yet and that snow will not just precipitate but may also bury us alive.

In addition to watching the dog, I am cutting up the eggplants to make a stew. I don't know how to make stew but I am trying. I see enough people do it on that cooking show.

If my mother were here, she would say, Put eggplant in stew, because in Chinese there are no articles.

In spoken Chinese, everything is gender neutral. There is no *she* or *he*. The more I think about this now, the more I like this about the language. Man or woman? Does it matter? A person.

Mao once said that women hold up half the sky.

. . .

I do have a cousin my own age. She grows up in China. When I visit at the end of high school, she has grown into a cool person.

The word for *cool* in Chinese she has to teach me.

You talk like your parents, she says. It is old-fashioned. She says this smugly, of course. She has to. That is the only way I will remember it for years to come and still feel the burning shame.

I am closest to my grandfather on my mother's side, though I have not seen him since I left. The last time we speak is when I am twelve and he is dying. I say that I will visit him tomorrow, don't worry, I will be there.

But before I see him again—that is, wait for the visa to come through and fly back to China—he dies.

In the same month, my other grandfather dies.

I used to tell Eric, You take for granted this distance, how close everyone is, a few hours' drive, from one relative to another and no need for a visa.

Which is how families are until one person decides to emigrate.

I'm sure my parents realized this possibility when they left, that returning would be hard.

By the time we make it to China, the funerals have already happened. My mother, grief-stricken, says that she will not be coming back with us. She will be staying in China with her mother.

There is much fighting over this, behind closed doors. That glow you see around a closed door is the property of diffraction. It is light trying to escape the room and move around an obstacle, in this case the door, my parents. I am scared sitting at the edge of my bed.

This is not just about you or me, he says, and stops there.

I have only one parent now, she says. She cries. She says something in Shanghainese. Maybe something like It has never been about me. Aren't you tired of this? Because I am. This I gather from her tone, the hiccupped way that she speaks when she cries. She must be tired. When the door finally opens, I watch her slump to the floor in a few steps.

Just recalling the way she collapsed, shoulders then knees, fills me with enormous guilt. On the plane back, I almost tell her, when we land, If you want to take the plane back, I wouldn't mind.

Why do you defend her? the shrink asks. She doesn't deserve this kind of loyalty.

Because mothers have parents too? Because they have lives beyond their own children?

Because I still want her to be happy.

Many times, she lifted up my chin and said, You must be better than the man you marry. You must succeed beyond him.

I cannot fail her too.

.   .   .

An equation.

happiness = reality − expectations
If reality > expectations, then you are happy.
If reality < expectations, then you are not.

Hence the lower your expectations, the happier you will be.

Once the psychologists behind the equation reached that conclusion, they stopped and put forth a caveat: No one should lead a life of low expectations. Emotions such as disappointment are also important to experience.

.   .   .

Little is known about the effects of long-term space travel. Though the primary concern is extreme loneliness.

I am an only child, I tell Eric.

It is an early date. We are at the International House of Pancakes again. I am eating a pancake called Funny Face and he is eating toast.

Something else in common, he says. He is an only child too.

But I am the only child of immigrants, and he looks at me, confused.

What difference does that make?

It's like deep space traveling.

To think, I once thought doing a chemistry PhD on top of that was a good idea.

What some people say about difficult experiences: If I could go back and do it again, I would.

No, I don't think so.

———

One newspaper article claims that elite American schools are good at producing only excellent sheep, the kind that can jump through hoop after hoop and not ask why.

The same goes for Asians, another article says. Give them a task and they will achieve it with high success. They will do everything you say, but ask them to think on their own and they cannot. They will also never ask why.

The best friend and the shrink say I should care less about what others think of me, so I have stopped reading those articles.

But still there are the remarks from people I have told about quitting the PhD but not telling my parents:

For once, stand up to them.

You just don't know how to stand up to them.

You cannot live your life for them. Eventually they will die, and then what?

At least the best friend and the shrink say none of that. One says, It's hard, I know, tell them whenever you're ready. The other hands me a box of tissues.

I am an excellent sheep.

But what I would give to be a spider right now. Where is an exoskeleton when you need it?

The movie *Stepmom* makes me cry as well. That movie is always playing on cable, and when I see that it's on, I must watch it to the end. The conversation between the two moms about the daughter in the penultimate scene makes me cry the most. One mom is dying of cancer and the other is the stepmom whom no one likes. The daughter is twelve and the mom dying of cancer is worried that on her daughter's wedding day, the daughter will forget her. The stepmom is worried too. She is worried that on this wedding day, the daughter will wish that she had her real mom by her side instead of her stepmom.

My mother has watched this movie many times. She watches it alone in her bedroom, the door slightly ajar. Does she cry during the penultimate scene? She would say no, never, yet she comes out of the bedroom with a tissue over her nose and declares it allergy season again.

What do you like about the movie? the shrink asks.

Not what. I like it because she does.

Advice from the mother: Hold yourself upright when you cry. If you cry lying down, tears will get into your ears and cause an infection.

When I shared this with Eric, he asked how on earth I still believed in that stuff.

That stuff, I said angrily, wanting to shake my fists in his face. Then did so.

Why does she deserve this kind of loyalty? She doesn't. But she does because she is my mother.

.   .   .

I discover that winter is here when I go outside with damp hair from a shower and in ten seconds my hair is frozen. There are viral videos of Boston kids doing something similar to test the cold. Except they soak a pair of jeans and then leave the jeans outside and then wait ten seconds for the jeans to freeze and stand up on their own.

Finally, the best friend hires a nanny because this is impossible, the long hours at the hospital and then the long hours at home. She thinks the nanny will give her peace of mind. But then at work, she is constantly wondering if the nanny is doing her job or just watching movies on their TV.

The nanny is young, and for a second, she worries about having one of those fiascoes on her hands. But the husband is so busy these days that he doesn't even notice the new person in the room until, hours later, he looks up from his laptop, is startled, thinks there's a stranger in the house.

While it is winter in Boston, it is summer in Antarctica. At the start of every session, the math student likes to give me the weather report from there.

It is summer but still unbelievably cold.

Negative 10 with wind gusts of up to sixty-five miles an hour.

Or negative 5 with the humidity of a desert.

Antarctica, I learn, is the driest place in the world despite being made up of ice. No, that is not true, he says, one percent of Antarctica is ice-free.

He shows me a picture of the girl and all I see is a red parka with fur lining and goggles.

She has a lovely mouth, I say. Surprisingly un-chapped, given the circumstances.

The picture he keeps in his wallet. It is an old pic-ture, he says. She has since cut her hair a dozen or so times.

What does her hair look like now? I ask.

He has to take a minute to recall. Short, he thinks. And wavy?

.   .   .

A hallmark of science is setting out to discover one thing and then discovering something else. The Chi-nese discovered gunpowder when they were trying to find the elixir of life. The four great Chinese inven-tions are gunpowder, paper, printing, and the compass.

But China is much more than that, I told Eric. It is both very old and very new. You will see what I mean when you visit.

And when would I do that? he replied. This was after the first time he had asked.

I don't know, I said, playing dumb. After you marry someone Chinese, I suppose.

On the coldest day of the year, I bike to the library cursing. I miss him most but sometimes I also miss the car, his attention, me climbing into the front seat with the heaters already blasting. At the library, I meet with student after student. It is tiring, the constant talking, writing, lifting of one's eyebrows to not look angry.

Are you doing a good job? asks the shrink, and I say I don't know. Also, how can you possibly know anything?

The shrink smiles. She thinks it's kind of funny when I try to out-shrink her.

I must not be doing a bad job because the woman who hired me wants to give me a raise. That's too much, I say. Who would pay that much?

Lots of people, it seems.

Is it four pizzas or five? I calculate and it's actually twenty-one pizzas an hour. The best friend calls me a rich lady.

A word problem about fruit: You have two apples and two bananas, but how many pineapples do you have?

I read the problem again. A trick of the mind that now keeps happening when I tutor the math student. He brings me a worksheet and I misread every problem.

Is this greater than or equal to pineapples?

Assume a six-sided pineapple, now pineapple, pineapple, pineapple.

Eventually, I tell the math student to look that way, at the girls dropping books and coffee, instead of at me, so that I can stop seeing pineapples.

. . .

Another task the shrink has given me: Do not forget the father. Recall him as well.

Here is what he said:

The sky is not blue or gray or white. It is the color of one septillion snowflakes falling to the ground. Septillion is one followed by twenty-four zeros, which is more zeros than you can write in one sitting because you are an impatient child. Now sit down, be quiet, and let me show you how to do math.

Multiply, divide, add, and then subtract, in that order because that is the order of operations and the way anything gets done. Here is an imaginary answer that does not exist until I write down the letter i and then it does, right there on the page. Here is a square root, a rational root, a reciprocal, a conjugate, a complex conjugate that is a pain to solve but you must do it anyway if you are to learn anything.

Play with your dolls for no more than half an hour, no more than fifteen minutes, no more than a second, a millisecond. If you learned math as fast as you ran outside to play, then you might be a genius. But you do not and you are not. You're a hole where knowledge goes to sleep.

Sit here and let me show you how to do physics. Without physics, you will be ignorant of the world. You will be empty, hollow, unable to articulate why, for instance, a rocket flies through the void your teachers call outer space. And why does a rocket fly in space?

I didn't know. I didn't even guess. How stupid of me. And he said that too, How stupid of you.

Wire your dollhouse and then you will understand electricity. Wire this bathroom light and then you will really understand electricity. Put the galvanometer here and here and don't shock yourself. See what happens when you don't listen to me? You've shocked yourself. Now stand up and try it again.

Again.

Again.

Again.

Listen for the Doppler effect or you will never understand sound, and if you never understand sound, then you will never understand melody or harmony or the reason a violin is shaped the way that it is.

If possible, come here and let me show you how real projectiles fly. Here is a stone that you must skip eleven times, no more, no less; you have to get your launch angle just right.

I threw the stone down. It skipped zero times. And he said, You are definitely no child of mine.

Do your taxes early. Pay your bills on time. Don't cheap out on your insurance. Open a 401(k). Open a high-interest savings account or don't and be poor for the rest of your life. Do you want to be poor?

No.

Then think hard about the children that you currently do not have because if they're anything like you, they'll want things that you do not have.

He said, On this birthday, you are now four thousand fifteen days old, and if you can tell me what the log of that is, then you can have some balloons. And if you can't figure out what I mean, then no balloons.

He said, Chew with periodicity. Don't just swallow it whole. Also, what is this idiom? To miss something by a hair?

I told him.

Ah, now calculate for me the width of that hair.

In the evenings, he said, Tell me the time. No, not like that. Tell me the time in arc second per second or don't tell me at all.

But even he had his superstitions.

Remember this, he said. A spider landing on your shoulder is good luck. A slug crawling across your hand is bad luck. Inspect your study site before you proceed. Sit down with care.

Dreams of teeth falling out mean sickness.

Dreams of white clothing mean death.

Dreams of fish means luck.

Unless they are dead fish.

Try not to dream.

Sharpen all your pencils with a knife. It is the best way to conserve lead.

This technique he has shown me. You want to

know how to get through life? Here's how you do it. You must keep your thumb on the blade and push down. You must push down forcibly. Your thumb will most likely hurt before the pencil is very sharp.

. . .

There is a new episode of the cooking show and a Chinese American chef is competing. She has electric-blue hair. She can do cool tricks with her knives. For these reasons, I drop everything to watch her cook.

All French food.

All delicious looking and expertly cut.

In between rounds, she talks about her upbringing. Her mother was very quiet. Her father was very strict. They expected certain things of her and cooking was not one of them. But here she is.

Ready to fight.

There is then a round of applause from the judges. Bravo, they say, to have found your own voice and rebelled.

But something about the way she tells her story frustrates me. Perhaps it is the broadness of her smile or how casually she dismisses them. And my mother is quiet like a lot of Asian mothers. And my father is strict like a lot of Asian fathers. And we are unhappy like a lot of Asian families.

I prevailed above all that, she makes excruciatingly clear. I am a chef and not a sheep.

It was the Chinese roommate who first said to me,

We are our own worst propagators of those clichés. We are constantly throwing each other under the bus.

But I am also angry at these judges. Why encourage this of us, to constantly rebel, without understanding why some of us do not?

.   .   .

With each passing car on this walk, I have stopped to hear the whooshing sound it makes.

That is the Doppler effect.

What Tolstoy said about unhappy families.

.   .   .

Tell me about the baby. How much has she grown? What shape are her fingernails? The length of her lashes? Send me a picture of the mole on her back. Two moles now? Send me a picture of the other one as well.

The best friend says that the baby is much improved, able to look at the thing she is pointing at instead of just the finger. Able to sense the passing of time and wonder the same thing she is wondering. Where is the father, the husband?

But isn't he always busy?

Yes, there is that and then there is something else she suspects.

Heisenberg's uncertainty principle states that to determine the precise location of a particle will only speed up the particle. The same goes for a husband: to ask him exactly where he has been all night will only make him squirm and wiggle and dodge the question more. He will only disappear again.

So the best friend has stopped asking.

In the college writing class I took, the instructor was very against writing what you know. Write what you don't know or write what you want to know.

So I wrote about a girl meeting a boy and them living happily ever after.

It cannot be that easy, he said, all over my margins, in all caps. Put in pain and struggle and any other obstacle that you can think of.

I had the girl chop the boy up and hide him in the walls.

I had the girl chop the boy up and fry him in hot oil.

At least it is not bland, he said. Next time, before she chops him up, have them talk to each other. The boy must know why.

For a few days, the best friend is reeling from the cliché of it. She would have first guessed the nanny, but it is a slightly different story. The husband has a new secretary. The new secretary has great breasts.

I must kill them both, she tells me. It is her newfound solution to everything. It is a surgeon's approach—if malignant, then cut. If benign, then leave.

In his defense, he says that the secretary with great breasts was not a cause but a symptom.

What did you say when he said that? I ask.

I didn't say anything. I threw the frying pan.

That's good. Always lead with the frying pan.

Something from the news: in China, a girl newly single and unhappy about it sits in a KFC for ten days before being coaxed out by the police.

Four nights in a row, I have the same dream. The husband is placed on a conveyor belt and sent into Earth's inner core. He comes back a bucket of fried chicken.

. . .

It is one of those sunless weeks. For seven straight days, the sky is gray like elephants. And then on the eighth day there is fog. I wonder if the sun has gone to Antarctica. For a couple of weeks in December, the continent sees sunlight for twenty-four hours a day.

The best friend is a bit distant these days and slower to return my texts. The mind is busy processing what the body feels.

Are you sobbing? I ask over text, and she says no.

But I am not allowed to ask her that question twice in one day or she sends back an angry emoji.

On a rare day off work, she calls and says, Entertain me. No more talk of the husband. A different topic: What's going on with your student? She and the baby are at a shopping mall. It's noisy, so I try to change the subject—Did you say something? Are you there? Sorry, but I can't hear you.

I don't like him in that way is my go-to line.

Why should I like him? is my other go-to line.

· · ·

One morning, while putting on my sweater, I realize that I have forgotten how to say *sweater* in Chinese. I panic all morning until I find my way to a dictionary.

Your face, my mother said, is entirely Chinese, so it is a prerequisite that you speak your mother tongue. Also, you are my daughter.

But what you don't speak often, you will eventually forget.

So I have started to talk to the dog in Chinese.

But the dog is having an identity crisis as well. There are times when he thinks he is a cat. Convincingly, he does the licking of the fur and the coughing up of fur and the arching of the back.

Stop that, I tell him, and repeat what Eric had firmly believed: that all cats are assholes.

Don't be an asshole.

The dog is also a sock lover. He has never been that interested in shoes. This, I am told at the dog park, makes me a lucky person. Each sock he finds he will ball up in his mouth and go from room to room presenting. He is doing it right now.

What do you have there? I ask, and must pry it out of his mouth.

It is not one of my socks. It is one of Eric's.

Where did you get this?

He rolls over.

Stop avoiding the question.

He keeps rolling over.

I end up putting the sock on the nightstand where I can see it. Whenever I see it, there is that soreness again.

The shrink calls this self-punishing.

In general, I have a hard time throwing out clothes, even when holes appear. I cannot throw away that blouse. I wore it to a party. I cannot throw away those pants. I wore them to the dentist. That shirt with a gash down its side, no, definitely not, I wore it on a hike with Eric and then it caught on a bush.

A possible reason for this behavior. What are girls wearing when I start going to school? Limited Too, Abercrombie, Gap. These clothes are expensive. My mother refuses to buy them. Here is when I realize that every penny is saved. It is not the studio we live in—a closet. It is not the food we eat—never Applebee's. As a child, I get new clothes so rarely that when I do, I put off wearing them. It then happens that when the big day finally comes, the clothes no longer fit.

.   .   .

In the middle of a sunless week, the best friend arrives unexpectedly. She is shivering when she arrives.

Just for a day or two, she says, until everything over there is in order.

They've been in the bedroom, she says, so the mattress must be burned.

In her hands, the baby, much bigger than I remembered. The eyes still black marbles, the skin now blush tint.

We skewer the husband first. He who cannot tie his own ties. He who will not change one diaper. He who smells of cigarette smoke, every day, toward the end. He who cannot cook worth a damn. We say *damn* quietly, while covering the baby's ears.

That is not true, she says after she has calmed down. He changed a lot of diapers. He tried to cook some things. Macaroni and cheese. Dino nuggets.

What do I do? she asks.

Leave him.

What else?

I think that's it.

I find the best friend asleep on the floor, curled up. She says the bed is too comfortable for what she is trying to accomplish.

Which is what?

To feel the hardness of something.

Is it working?

I don't know. Everything hurts.

If she has cried, she has not done so in front of me. She has done so in the shower where it is hard to tell.

Together we watch movies late into the night. Only movies with long car chases and explosions and fist-fights are allowed. Movies like *Mad Max*. We like *Mad Max*. The more machine guns the better. None of that sissy stuff, we say.

The baby is on the same page and has been nick-named the Destroyer of Small Things. She takes everything out of our wallets and then throws it on the floor.

The best friend says to the Destroyer, Can you please go away for thirty seconds and come back a sweeter child?

The Destroyer nods while pounding our empty wallets flat.

The next day, they are back in New York City. There is no clothes flinging or hand-wringing or second frying pan.

Take nothing, she tells the husband, just vanish.

· · ·

Proverbs about the sky:

Do not look at the sky from the bottom of a well.

If you are willing to take a step back, there is boundless sky.

I wonder if I should call him again, but it never goes beyond that. I try not to say his name or think it, but it's such a common name. I go into a CVS and see the air freshener brand Air Wick and leave without buying anything.

Also, there is that famous Jimi Hendrix lyric; he said, *Excuse me while I kiss the sky,* which always gets confused with *Excuse me while I kiss this guy.*

In differential geometry, two curves are said to kiss when they share the highest possible number of contacts.

The first time he and I kiss, it is outside my old apartment building. He is waiting for a cab. I am waiting to be kissed. Our teeth clank because we are smiling too much beforehand. Then he blushes and tells me about Jimi Hendrix.

The ancient Chinese were also enthralled with the sky. They attempted to catalog every single star but showed little interest in planets.

At the edge of our galaxy, there is said to be a planet made out of diamonds. This was quickly disputed. It isn't diamonds. It is graphite. The thing inside every pencil. The atomic difference between diamond and graphite is nothing. They are both made out of carbons. The carbons are just arranged differently.

The song "Lucy in the Sky with Diamonds" he doesn't care for. He knows why his former bandmates like it. A simple melody on top of a complex chord progression, a time signature change from the verses (in three) to the chorus (in four), which is a baller move, he adds, for 1967. But overall he finds the song kind of silly. Then the long-standing controversy over the title. Of course, they were high, he says.

Did you love him? the shrink asks.

I almost laugh at such a straightforward question.

But did you tell him? Did you say it out loud?

. . .

Aerial perspective is what happens when things in the distance look cooler, more blue. It is a way to create the illusion of depth in any painting.

How did we get on the topic of painting? I ask the math student, who doesn't know either.

He brings me a plate of olives.

He brings me a bowl of nuts.

When I am not chomping on all of those things, we learn a little bit of math. To remember your trig, recite Soh Cah Tah. To remember you colors, recite Roy. G. Biv.

The next day, I decide to paint my bedroom some kind of blue. It has always been white but the starkness is just now getting to me. I go to the store where we bought the fan and look around, but the paint colors are infinite and confusing.

What is sapphireberry?

What is Adriatic mist?

I stumble across a color called sea sprite and try to joke with the man behind the counter.

See spite. Get it? You know *see,* with two *es.* And *spite,* that angry feeling?

He says he gets it.

If Eric were here, I think he would have laughed.

In the end I like the sound of permafrost. I will surround myself with four walls of it. When the best friend comes to help me paint, she is less convinced. Are you sure about the color? Isn't it already pretty bad out?

The Destroyer tries to help as well. She sticks a finger in her yogurt cup and smears a little on the wall, then looks at us deviously, then smears a little more on herself. By the time the room is painted, we have to get the yogurt-covered baby into the tub. But she is also anti-water. Once we do get her into the tub, we must speed-wash her before the thrashing gets too out of control.

Chinchillas clean themselves in a shallow bed of sand. They don't ever go near water. Maybe the baby is secretly a chinchilla. We take her to an indoor playground with a sandbox and it doesn't seem to be the case.

From a TV documentary on Antarctica, I learn that you cannot work there unless you have both your wisdom teeth and appendix removed. There are very few full-time dentists. There are very few physicians.

Fifty-three million years ago, palm trees grew along the shores.

Now there is ice a mile deep.

A volcano that spews crystals.

No polar bears, just penguins and fifteen hundred different species of fungi.

I don't think I am teaching him math anymore. All we do sometimes is look up videos of penguins doing clumsy things.

At the end of each session, he gives me a good-bye hug. He takes to putting his chin on top of my head during our good-bye hugs.

It feels nice, having some pressure up there.

Did you know, he asks, that oxygen is sky blue colored when frozen?

I did but say that I didn't.

. . .

The husband vanishes. By vanish, she meant seek out one of your finance buddies and crash with him until further notice. Do not try to contact me. Do not call my friend in Boston and have her relay a message. He listens. He leaves her alone. For a while, she is not so livid.

But then a month later, in January, she sees the secretary at a doughnut shop, and, livid again, she digs through her purse for something sharp. Her stethoscope. Is it wise to kill someone with an instrument of health? She decides against it, storms out, runs straight to another coffee shop, and calls me.

How do you know it was her? I ask.

Because she has looked up the secretary extensively. She has gone through every online picture of her available. Not only great breasts, it seems, but also a winning smile.

I decide it is better to listen and say nothing. The best friend has begun to talk in that hopeless, breathless way of the estranged.

The husband is gone.

He's gone, she says.

What Mad Max said: The chain in those handcuffs is high-tensile steel. It'd take you ten minutes to hack through it with this. Now, if you're lucky, you could hack through your ankle in five minutes.

When we got to that part in the movie, we agreed that Mad Max must also be married.

Silly things we now say to each other: Don't be such a Debbie Downer. Don't be such a Wet Nancy.

The last one I said by mistake when I was trying to remember that phrase about blankets.

Why are all the sad idioms about girls? she asks—a fair point, but neither of us knows.

·   ·   ·

The weather people were not kidding about the snow. Inches turn into feet and under the white mounds are cars and buses and doorways. Also, the air hurts my face. Why do I live in a place where the air hurts my face?

When here, the baby does not always like to sit still and eat her food. So I am trying something new. I stick rice on the baby's face in the shape of palm trees and clouds. I make a banana slice sun.

The baby sits incredibly still for this and then, giggling, while looking at herself in a mirror, eats the landscape off her face.

But the trees are all white, says the best friend.

Ignore your mother. They're clearly palm trees covered in snow.

On one hand I am playing tug with the dog, on the other I am smoothing out the baby's hair. The moment comes when we can put the hair up into a one-inch ponytail and the best friend has a look of shock. This is the most incredible thing ever, she says, hands around the head.

This good moment is followed by a bad one, when we go shopping and the best friend passes a lingerie store. She stops and stares at the large posters of models.

This is all your fault, she says to one of the posters. You did this to him, you and your female wiles. Then she moves on to next poster. I follow and apologize to each woman in turn.

Sorry, my friend is not quite herself today.

You would like her normally.

I understand, all this is just a job.

When she is done with the posters, she sits down on the ground. Secretly, I am envious, she says. I want it all. To be smart and beautiful, physically beautiful. It is vain, I know, but that is what I want.

There were times when I told my father, All you want me to do is study, all you want me to do is achieve. I am tired of learning everything.

What use is all this knowledge when in school they are still calling you a freak?

I could not tell that in his questions, the many times he motioned me over to teach me one of the three things, was his desire for me to be fearless.

Is being fearless better than being pretty?

My mother, for all her looks, marries my father, who is not handsome. When they meet, she must see something different in him. He is serious, often too serious, and she finds this intriguing or maybe endearing. If he is going to make it abroad, he tells her, he is going to get a PhD. At the time, my mother thinks, A PhD, what is that? No one around her is getting one, much less thinking of doing it abroad.

The face, the body, my mother refers to these things as hardware. You cannot change them. But you can change what you know and the mind, she refers to as software.

Though is that true? There is makeup, surgery, weight loss. Hardware is easily changeable nowadays.

Beauty is weakness, I remember a model saying during an interview. She is referring to when people see how gorgeous she is; they immediately think that she is not strong.

But I think my mother would have had a harder time here if she were not beautiful. When she arrives, she begins using beauty as a shield. She does not enjoy being poor (who does?), but she manages, adopts a saying: If you are beautiful, you will look good in anything, even this shabby little number from Kmart. Also, what does she have now if not beauty? There is her wit, but how to get across wit in a language she does not speak?

My mother is not dumb. She knows beauty is not everlasting. So she tells me often, You are not beautiful, do not think yourself beautiful, and I am angry at her for a long time.

It is a double-edged sword.

To be smart and beautiful, says the best friend, and this is probably very close to what every woman wants. I too had high hopes of growing up into both a genius and a bombshell.

To be Marie Curie but then to also look like Grace Kelly.

.   .   .

Born Maria Salomea Skłodowska, she is the first to win two Nobels. She is the first to win it in two different sciences. In 1902, she isolates one-tenth of a gram of a new chemical and discovers radioactivity. Pierre, her husband, calls the new chemical radium, from the Latin word *radius,* meaning ray.

Once, Eric and I debated who was the best chemist of all time. He said these things were hard to quantify, what metric do you use?

How about just the sheer number of metals? I said.

How about just the sheer number of discoveries?

But why does there have to a best? he asked. Why does there have to a worst?

Chemistry, while powerful, is sometimes unpredictable. In 1902, radium's glow is mistaken for spontaneous energy and Marie is celebrated. But then in 1928, the lip-pointing girls, the going straight to your bones.

.   .   .

Do you have a very smart dog? asks other owners after I tell them that he prefers socks.

I think so. Then they tell me of a test to see if you truly have a smart dog. Put a blanket over the dog and see how long it takes him to get out of it.

I do this and start the timer.

But the dog is so immobilized by the darkness—Oh my god, the darkness, the world has disappeared before my eyes—that at the four-minute mark, he lies down.

Another test is to put a treat under a plastic cup and see how long it takes him to get the treat out.

A week later, the cup is still there.

I give him the treat anyway. It's okay. You don't have to be a very smart dog. I actually prefer that you're not. If you were a very smart dog, I wouldn't find you as funny.

At the end of a recent session, the math student asks if I have somewhere to be after this (not really), if we are saying good-bye now (I don't know), let's go somewhere else (sure, okay). We stroll through a park. We play a game. How many cars are buried under that snow pile? Two or a billion? I tell him that proverb, then I tell him this joke: If you start digging it is cars all the way down.

Likes? Dislikes? We sit in a café and talk about how we both hate to bowl and then go bowling the day after, thinking that the other person is terrible, but then, at the bowling alley, find out that the other person is not terrible at all and was in fact putting up a ruse.

He is quite competitive.

I am a terrible loser.

He puts an arm around my shoulders anyway. I notice that his arm span is much longer than Eric's and thicker, so more insulating against the wind. But I do not feel much safer. I feel about the same.

.   .   .

Ping goes my computer when a new e-mail comes in. Actually the computer is silent. The *ping* is in my head. It is an e-mail from Eric.

But I'm not going to open it, I say. At least not until tomorrow.

Then tomorrow comes and I decide not to open it until the day after.

Open it right now, says the best friend, whom I page at work again, asking what I should do.

It could be important, she says. What if he is trying to tell you something? What if someone in his family died? Open it right now.

I can't.

Accidentally or not, I hit delete. Then I panic. Where did it go? In the time that I search through my phone, it feels as if my eyes have fallen out of my head and rolled elsewhere.

You have to write him back, she says, or else he will think that you don't care.

But he already thinks that. And maybe I should let him continue to think that and move on and find someone else. Maybe this is all for the best because he deserves someone equally good, if not gooder.

Gooder?

I mean goodest.

The best friend says, At the very least, write him an e-mail to say that you are alive.

————

I place bets with myself while biking.

If I catch three green lights in a row, I will write him back today.

If I catch no green lights, I will write him back sometime later.

A universal law of traffic: once you hit one red light, you will hit them all.

If I'm not going to write that e-mail I might as well exercise. At midnight, I do jumping jacks. The online fitness guru has a new move. It is called the mountain climber froggy hop.

The what? I say, while trying to do it.

Afterward, I make myself a health smoothie. I put in blueberries, a plum. Looking at the purple blender, I turn on some music: Jimi Hendrix. I turn the volume up high.

He said, You look pretty in a *qipao*. You are prettier than manganese. But the challenge is to be both smart and pretty, so I push his compliments away because I think believing them will mean that I have compromised.

My singing is terrible. *Purple haze, all in my brain.*

Soon the people downstairs complain. They call the landlord who then calls me. What is that terrible ruckus?

I remember something else he said. The song's intro, weirdly discordant. A tritone. A flat five. Sometimes called the devil's interval. It is the guitar and bass, playing the same octave pattern but with different notes. The guitar plays a B flat; the bass plays an E.

. . .

The baby has become sentient. When we walk, she screams across the street at other babies, baby expletives, we think. Something along the line of God-damn it, other baby, don't try to out-cute me. To make matters worse, she is very cute, so we have a hard time correcting her.

In another life, the baby might have been a spider monkey or a possum. She likes to be held upside down and up high. She likes to be able to touch her feet to the ceiling.

A recent development: at the end of each workday, the husband calls and leaves a long-winded voice message. The best friend plays me these messages. They are truly long-winded.

I'm sorry. I miss you. I'm sorry. I miss you. Would you ever consider coming back and visiting for a little while, just as a friend?

He says our daughter, I don't know how many times.

What do we think? she asks. Isn't he being redundant? Why is he being so redundant? What do we think?

We think this is okay? We think life is so ambiguous.

Light interacting with itself is called interference. Colorful spots appear when light builds on itself, one wave adding to another, like five plus five equals ten. The dark spots appear when light destroys itself, one wave negating the other, like negative five plus five equals zero.

To students I say, Observe the surface of an oil slick or a bubble. See how an entire fluorescent rainbow lives there, see how the colors change, fan out, the red violets and golds. You could not get such patterns if light didn't struggle internally as well.

And if they don't believe me, I will take them to the nearest gas station and show them an oil slick.

During one of our strolls, I take the math student to see the oil slick as well.

It is not really a test.

But it is sort of a test. My wondering if he would appreciate it. He is quiet for a moment but then points to a spot of orange and calls it tangerine.

. . .

My mother's mother was one of the best architects in Shanghai.

In the late 1970s, she helps reconstruct the Bund. During this time, she tells my mother, still a teenager, that if she were ever to settle down and have children, she need only have daughters. Daughters have more *chu xi* and *xiao shun,* she says. *Chu xi* is the ability to succeed. *Xiao shun* is filial piety. My grandmother believes this because she was one of those daughters— having accomplished a great deal, having married well, raised two kids, and taken care of her parents in the last years of their lives.

But to follow my father to America, my mother inevitably gives up both.

And for this reason, I think she believes herself to have failed.

Then the moment of shock set in. A daughter? You must be mistaken. I do not have a daughter. And if I did, how would I raise her if I cannot set for her an example?

Upon putting that car in reverse and leaving, she thinks, Finally, a chance to start anew. But then she realizes that she cannot get very far without my father. There are many things she cannot read or say. And money, she doesn't have her own money.

Maybe she also comes back because of you, the shrink says. The maternal instinct kicking in.

If she does, she never shows it. I am home from school and see her shoes at the door. I don't need to look very far. She is back in the bedroom calling China.

During the fight after the French restaurant, I try to explain to Eric why I didn't want to get married. I say, I don't want to be congratulated for being married.

He says getting married is a normal thing to do. Also, what's so wrong about being congratulated?

Nothing, theoretically.

I should have explained it another way. *Chu xi,* do you know that word? I don't want to be someone without any.

But how could he have understood? His parents have a happy marriage. He grows up in a happy home.

For a moment, I let myself imagine it. Us in a big house in Ohio, a yard for the dog to run in. I can't quite imagine it. It is too happy.

At some point my mother, probably to comfort me, tells me that there is no good marriage without constant fighting. Fighting is how a husband and wife talk.

One time, my father accuses her of running off to be with another man. She laughs at this.

Who would I go with? she says. Who would want to be with me in the long run?

The shrink says that whenever I go back into the past, I see only the bad.

But isn't that obvious? There is so much bad.

That cannot be entirely true.

What is the scientific method? A physics teacher. High school. He speaks theatrically. It is a method that leads us to truth. Then in college, another professor. Science is not a panacea; activities such as human interactions are difficult to answer with this method.

———

The Shanghainese word for maternal grandmother is *ah bu*. She teaches me this. I do not know it is a Shanghainese word until I say it to the Chinese roommate—My *ah bu* was once an architect, my *ah bu* lives in Shanghai—and she says, What is an *ah bu*? You mean that monkey from *Aladdin*?

. . .

The city has made the record books. February sees the most snowfall in a century. On every news channel, there is a montage of miserable people shoveling snow but happy kids because school has been canceled for weeks.

Some people have taken to bottling the snow and sending it to California residents who are in desperate need of water. When asked how much of the snow removal budget we have gone through, the mayor just says, Thank god it is March.

Over the phone, I hear the baby cry and cry. Teething. The best friend has locked herself in the bathroom temporarily and slid down into the tub.

What am I doing? she says.

We talk about something else—Your student, okay not that, Eric, not that either, then what are we going to talk about?

Let's talk about you, you warrior mom you.

A minute later, she is ready to go back out there.

This piece of advice from the Internet: At the end of the day have any of your children been eaten by wolves? No? Then you're a good mother.

.   .   .

But March is also frigid.

At T.J. Maxx, I find a face mask. The kind that covers the entire face except for the eyes, the mouth, and could allow me to rob banks. I say aloud, These things exist? And for $3.99?

I purchase it and wear it home. My face no longer feels like an ice sheet. I can feel that I still have a nose. Soon, I start to notice other people with face masks, mostly fellow bikers, trudging up the same hills that I am. I wave to one. I give another a thumbs-up.

Maybe I could go back to lab this way, with a face mask, and start again.

During our walks, the dog thinks he is also walking me. Must exercise human, he thinks, must get human out of the house, and then he happily leads me around the park. He does not go up to everyone, but everyone he has gone up to has been offering goods. During a spontaneous hailstorm, a woman gives us her umbrella.

I don't live that far from here, she says. But save the dog. That beautiful coat must not get ruined.

Then she dashes home and so do we, with me holding the umbrella over the dog.

But on the dash home, the hailstorm stops. The sun appears. And the dog put on the brakes to look for the sunniest spot to lie down. He picks the puddle at the intersection of two roads while I stand there and direct cars to go around us.

A proverb: My barn having burned down, I can now see the moon.

To progress in life, I still feel as if I must colonize the moon.

The shrink sighs. Why the moon? That's just setting yourself up for failure. I mean, yes, you should at least try, but don't kill yourself over it. There are other things out there.

Eric's childhood: long hours filled with chemistry sets and mercury thermometers and building the world's most advanced paper planes. A precocious child, a highly thoughtful yet meticulous one, and his parents wonder if this is normal. They try to get him to go outside and play ball, play catch, play with the other kids, and he does this sometimes but usually he is inside testing a fleet of paper planes, until one can finally bank properly and fly the length of his room.

Did your father teach you how to make them? I asked.

And he looked at me oddly. No. He had made them himself.

I now see the sense of discovery he must have had

when doing anything in lab. He was a fast and proficient chemist and so was I. The shrink says she doesn't question that.

But what every scientist knows—you can't just be proficient; you have to have insight.

·   ·   ·

Instead of cheese and crackers and a weather report, today the math student brings me breaking news. The Antarctica girl is no more.

What? I say, concerned. Did she perish into the ice?

Nothing like that, he says.

But there will be no more pictures in the wallet. There will be no more secret yearning. They will be friends, period.

Should I be feeling more at this moment? A sudden sense of levitation?

He says he can no longer be my student and I ask why.

·   ·   ·

We go bowling since it is clear we still cannot spend much time outside. But soon we get tired of bowling. Or I do, because he is hands down the better bowler.

How about this, I suggest, come over and we will shovel some snow. In the middle of March there is a tiny blizzard. The weather experts say *tiny* so that the

city will be less alarmed but everyone is thinking it—
I would rather live in tornado country than this place.

Also, the driveway needs salting. And the laundry
room door needs thawing. It has been frozen shut
from the outside.

I didn't think he would actually agree.

And arrive so punctually, with snow pants and goggles and gear.

Two shovels.

A bag of blue salt for the driveway.

A hair dryer for the door.

We are saved by that hair dryer. What would you
have done instead? the math student asks. Not wash
anything until spring?

I suppose? Or climbed in through the window.
Somehow both those options seemed more reasonable
than trying to melt the door.

But the dog is eternally grateful.

He quickly falls asleep with his head on the math
student's foot and the foot goes numb and we are stuck
in this position on the couch.

Hands not touching, but shoulders, yes.

. . .

It is as if we had not shoveled. The next day, the city
says, Here, have some more snow.

. . .

The baby has picked up some choice phrases. She can now point to the dog's butthole and say, Boo-boo. When we present her with a Band-Aid, she will try to put it over the hole and, if the dog runs, crawl after him until he submits.

I am letting her get away with so much, the best friend says. I am letting her pull my hair out of their roots. I am giving her the last bite of pie. What if she grows up too strong-willed?

I think a little strong-willed is okay.

The best friend has gone back and reanalyzed his proposal. Maybe the problem started there. It was very plain, she says, like an agreement between two people. We sat down and talked about it. Then we went out and got the ring.

But isn't that what you wanted? I ask.

She says yes, then no.

Maybe it was me, she says, during one of our movie-watching marathons.

It wasn't.

Maybe it was.

But you didn't do anything.

That's my point.

She cites the studies. A large number of new mothers get enough emotional fulfillment from holding their baby that physical contact with the significant other becomes less necessary.

Things like kissing, hugging.

Sex.

But he cheated on you.

And the best friend has a far-off gaze. Then she says, At full term, my belly button protruded. He would press it often and say, Eject. Afterward, I didn't let him touch it.

That's different.

It's the same. Every time he came close, I moved.

.   .   .

When you push against a wall, the wall pushes back on you. This is the most common way I've heard Newton's third law be described.

But I say to my students, Forget walls, think rockets. Newton's third law is why rockets fly in space. When a rocket shoots out a plume of fuel, the plume pushes back and the rocket goes forth.

In 1999, NASA lost a $125 million Mars lander. Instead of meters, they calculated the distance in feet, but the lander still interpreted this number in meters. Three feet make up a meter, so you can imagine, instead of landing on Mars softly, the lander crashed into the planet like a missile, thinking the distance was three times as far as it should have been.

Eric told me this story and now I use it to drive home the importance of units. He said it was his favorite space mission disaster to tell because at least no one died.

But someone might have gotten very, very fired.

See how important units are, I say to students. You do not want Martians to think you're an idiot.

I can't believe I used to do this: get mad at him for being a good person.

A lost package addressed to a house five blocks from us and he walks the five blocks to deliver it. A mistake on our grocery receipt—we got too much change back—and he runs back to the store to return it.

But we could have used that for laundry, I said, and he said, It would not have been right.

At the same time, at any hot food bar, I will take a piece of chicken tender and stick it in my mouth.

I used to call his being a better person than me condescension. You look down at me from that thing—what is that thing called? what did I call it then?—your moral fucking pedestal.

And he said, You know how every cloud has a silver lining? You are the cloud with the dark lining.

I am not a cloud, I shouted. I don't want to be a cloud.

One of my students has asked if clouds are made up of hydrogen, as hydrogen is the lightest element known to man.

Good reasoning, I replied. But if clouds were made of hydrogen, they would explode. See the *Hindenburg* incident. Hence why blimps are now filled with helium, the second-lightest element known to man, and so are balloons.

This student has since graduated from college and no longer needs my help, but we still keep in touch.

Whenever I think of clouds, she says, or balloons, I think of you.

To my surprise, most of my students keep in touch. I find in my inbox the occasional greeting. Hi, teacher, some of them still say. I am well. I am doing this now. I am reminded of you by many things.

Clouds
Balloons
A running faucet
A satellite
Mirrors
Baseballs
Bubbles
A sunset
A closed door
A full moon
Rocket ships
Chocolate
Glow-in-the-dark anything
A green laser
A green leaf
Teeth
White light

An oil slick
A spoon

Put that way, I don't mind being a cloud.

.   .   .

Eric spends one Christmas with my family. My mother cooks plate after plate of food. If they cannot understand each other, at least she will make sure that he is fed. At breakfast, she brings him a piece of toast. A minute later, a plate of bacon, a bowl of cereal, apple slices, scrambled eggs, string cheese. She has seen the commercials. What this means? Part of a balanced breakfast. She assumes a balanced American breakfast must then be very large.

He eats everything he can. Between meals all he can do sometimes is digest.

I forget this but remember it now: after I put the stapler down, I hear him go into the kitchen and say to her, The sun is here; the moon is there; look, a door! and then I hear her laugh in a giddy way.

Other things that make her laugh. Jokes. Especially terrible ones. How do you get an elephant into an elevator? You pick him up and put him in there. How do you get an elephant out of an elevator? You don't. You take the stairs.

During one of her good moods, she buys me a refrigerator magnet from a convenience store. The magnet says BEST DAUGHTER, she tells me, and I nod. I can't bring myself to tell her that it says BEST DOGSITTER.

At first glance the two words are very close. At second, practically indistinguishable.

Two Shanghainese words: *Ma zi. Ah zi.* One means sock and the other means shoe. I could never get them straight and my mother found this funny.

Forget dogsitter. Dog *mom.* To a woman at the dog park I say that I have cured my dog of vacuum cleaner phobia.

How? the woman asks.

By not vacuuming. By instead waiting for dust to accumulate in all corners of the room and then using the silent dustpan. I say a too-clean house gives me the heebie-jeebies. If you saw my parents' house, you would understand. It looks unlived in and beige.

To the dog, I say, If I am dog mom, then you are dog son. If you were a Japanese dog, I would say dog-san.

I have brief windows of clarity when I see that happiness is not just achievement but made up of many other things.

Like:

Finding keys, wallet, gloves (both of them) in a decent amount of time.

Finding leash—where is leash, where is poop bag, where is dog son?—in a decent amount of time.

Meeting another dog-human pair while waist deep in snow.

Watching dogs bound through snow.

Freezing our faces but not willing to stop dogs from bounding through snow.

Signs. I used to not believe in signs. But now I am all about them. At coffee shops when asked for a name to write on the cup, I accidentally give them his.

You're Eric? says one dubious barista, and I say, Yes, I mean no, then I give her the math student's name, then I give her the name Joy.

. . .

It comes as a small shock when she tells me. You're what?

Going into counseling.

What happened to take nothing and vanish?

But when she's older, she will have questions. People don't just vanish.

Amelia Earhart.

It's just once a week, she says. He still lives elsewhere. Nothing is decided yet.

Gut courage that transcended the sanity of reasoning. This is what another pilot said of Amelia Earhart.

When the best friend walks into counseling and

sees the husband, she sees the carpets, the drapes, the sofa, everything in the room catch on fire at once and there is much yelling.

To him, she keeps saying the words *How could you?* It has become a nervous tic.

She calls me. I call her. Both of us stand in front of mirrors late at night brushing our hair with our phones held between cheek and shoulder. When we are temporarily not talking about how badly her sessions go, she asks about Eric—had I heard from him again?

No.

Had I written him back?

No.

Had I tried anything?

No. And don't look at me like that.

I can't see her but I know that she is looking at me like that. I feel faint all of a sudden. Probably because I have forgotten how to breathe. How do you do it again?

You know, she adds quietly, he was also completely devoted to you. That should count for something.

The way she said that just now makes me think that she has been keeping it from me for a while.

. . .

In Chinese, there is another phrase about love. It is not used for passionate love but the love between family members. In translation, it means I hurt for you.

My mother says this while standing in the doorway of my bedroom because I have just asked why she
couldn't be more like the mothers of my American
friends, why she couldn't be affectionate like them. She
then holds a hand to her heart and says that the Chinese keep their feelings in here and not—she points to
air—out in the open. Now, I think, if she knew the
right idiom, she would have pointed to her sleeve.

I remember how my father learns English. We have
just left China. We are living in that studio. When
he comes back from work, he sits down on the floor
because there is no desk. He reads from the dictionary.
He learns ten new words a day.

In high school, I find his PhD thesis on the shelf.
I don't make it past the first page. The first page is
a dedication. For my wife and daughter, it starts and
then continues on in perfect English.

I have probably read that page a thousand times. I
have run my fingers across it.

A story my mother tells me when I am in college:

Your father, as a boy, carried his youngest sister on
his back to see the doctor. The doctor was many miles
away. The sister was dying of consumption. He ran on
dirt roads, as fast as he could. But before they could
get to the doctor, the sister died. Still he carried her to
the doctor's.

When I hear this story, I am stunned. But why had
he never mentioned the sister before? Why am I learning about her just now? If I knew about her earlier,
maybe I would have understood him more. The need

to succeed, to be fearless. But it is the Chinese way to not explain any of that, to keep your deepest feelings inside and then build a wall that can be seen from the moon.

Fast-forward a few years. I have just moved in with Eric. I have just gotten the dog. I want to tell everyone about the dog. But I am nervous to take him back to Michigan because I think my father will be annoyed. He has never shown an interest in animals before. Also, what a dog would do to their beige house.

When he first meets the dog, I cannot read his face. It is a blank face. But everywhere he goes, the dog follows.

He allows him on the hardwood but not on the carpet. He allows him on the carpet but not on the couch. When the dog cries at night from fear of being alone, he sleeps next to him on the floor.

. . .

A store that sells things I want but don't need lures me in. It has small gifts and charms. It has an aluminum paperweight in the shape of a heart. I pick it up. I put it down. I imagine my life with it. I leave the store. The same sequence every time.

Aluminum used to be more expensive than gold. Napoleon had an aluminum cutlery set that he used only for visiting royalty. The gold set he used every day.

Finally, I just buy it and take to walking around the apartment with it in my pocket.

What's this? the best friend asks when she gets an identical one in the mail.

A heart.

I know that, but what am I supposed to do with it?

Whatever you want.

She actually uses it as a paperweight, but then the baby finds it and gums all over it.

For the most part, she is a straight-faced baby. Until anyone starts ripping paper in front of her and then she can't help herself. It is all too funny.

Provide a stream of commentary for your baby, says all the how-to books. So I give it a try when they visit.

Here's a clean diaper so you will feel nice and dry. Here is another clean diaper because you pooped yourself as I was putting on your first one. Now I am buttoning your shirt—one, two, three buttons—and pulling up your fuzzy white pants. Shall we read a book next? If so, which one? How about the one with all the bears? You shaking your head like that tells me you are not liking any of these bears.

Shall we eat? Is that a yes?

How about I just start ripping paper like this so you can laugh.

You laughed too hard.

Here is another clean diaper.

A cheeky how-to book says for the first few months you are just trying to keep the baby alive. Then for the next several years, you are just trying to keep the baby from harming itself.

So the best friend has also become her savior—Don't touch that. Don't eat that. Don't put your whole fist in your mouth and try to swallow.

There are not many pictures of my mother and me when I was this age. We did not have a camera then.

But here is one.

She is holding me up on the coffee table to dance. We are both wearing ten layers of clothes. This must have been winter in China, when we also didn't have any indoor heat. We are smiling though.

Say cheese, I am later taught to do. School photos. Class photos. Photos with new friends. In China, we say the word for eggplant. It lifts the corners of the mouth in the same way.

. . .

The shrink unearths a true statement: Without your parents, you lose contact with everyone else in your family.

She means the ones who are still in China, which is everyone except for us.

I reply, I would try to keep in touch if I could. I would write or visit. I would definitely call.

But then on the way home, I realize that I have no

phone numbers or addresses. And even if I did, what would I say to these people who are my family but whom I have met only a handful of times. If I went by myself I would not know what to say. I could follow the conversation, but I could not retort or banter. It is true what Eric said about the humor being lost.

Before I leave for college, my parents buy a house. Every penny saved has bought them a two-story with a yard, a brick facade, in a nice neighborhood.

Jia is the Chinese word for home.

So wrapped up am I in the notion of being gone that I don't notice what they are trying to do.

My mother says: It is important to your father that you have a *jia*.

My father says: It is important to your mother that you have a *jia*.

But the house still needs renovations.

To cut costs, he does all the renovations himself. He rewires everything. He puts in a new heater, new floors, crown molding, light fixtures that my mother picks out. He builds an entirely new deck. She wallpapers each room, lining up the end of one scroll with the beginning of another. They work late into the night. She hands him tools and helps him lift the ladder. She puts down the tarp on which the ladder will go.

There is a funny online video I am now remembering. In China, a team of reporters had asked college students to call their parents and tell them I love you. For all, it was the first time they had done so. The responses:

Uh-huh.
Are you pregnant?
Are you drunk?
I am stepping into a meeting now.

But then one student says I love you again.
Why are you telling me this? asks the mother.
Because I love you.
And the mother, rather stoically, says, This is the happiest day of my life.

These words come back to me:
You cannot live your life for them. Eventually they will die.
I hope they never die because once they do, I will be alone.

. . .

In April, the snow finally starts to melt.
The Chinese word for chemistry is *hua xue*. The first character means to change, transform, melt. The second character means to learn. Said with a different inflection, *xue* could mean snow, *hua* could mean

speech and chemistry becomes the melting of snow, becomes the learning of speech.

All of May it rains. When I have to go out for food or the mail, I look angrily up at the sky.

It rains when it is sunny. Is that even a thing?

Apparently, they are called sun-showers.

When it finally stops raining, we are able to go out.

But the dog is Velcro. Every pollen or stem or leaf that falls from flowering trees sticks to him. So I spend, I think, an hour each day pulling plant life off him.

You silly thing, I say. So attractive.

He might actually be a very smart dog. What else would explain this: my peeling a banana and him smelling it from two rooms away, then appearing at my feet and looking at me, inching closer and closer, until I have handed over the fruit.

.   .   .

The best friend calls to tell me something. She is back in the bathtub.

Again?

Just for a minute, she says. Though it has become one of the only places where she can think. It is the first hot day in New York. It is the first hot day in Boston. Everyone in these cities is outside except for us.

The something she calls to tell me: We're old, she says. Also, she is now the same age she first remembers her mother being.

Isn't that strange?

It then strikes me that I am now the age when my father began sending those letters. I am now the age when my mother decided to go with him.

What courage.

If I had to leave America now, I would be terrified. There is the fear that I will not like this new place and vice versa. There is also the fear that I will never truly fit in and be forever getting in and out of cabs.

I call her immediately.

Mom, are you there?

Where else would I be? she says.

I say nothing about the courage. I say I was just checking my phone's signal.

The longest phone call we have is during the opening ceremonies of the Beijing Summer Olympics. The sheer number of people on that stage, the very long history of that country. My country? More so her country. It is four hours of colorful costumes and drums and calligraphy. I am watching it from lab and she is watching it from home. But during the call, we say very little to each other. What is there to say? I am thinking the whole time that this is incredible, how did the Chinese pull this off, how is anyone going to top this? I am immensely proud.

The online fitness guru talks often about core strength. The idea is that once you have a strong enough core, you can do all these ridiculously hard moves with a smile on your face.

The shrink says something similar, but she refers to it as inner strength.

Biologically, physical strength comes from mito-chondria, which are organelles that generate all of our body's energy. A unique feature of mitochondria is that they have their own DNA. Whereas the rest of the body is built on code that is half paternal and half maternal, mitochondrial DNA is entirely maternal and passed down from the mother.

· · ·

I know the tutoring is not permanent. I know I cannot do it long-term. But I like it and am not bad at it.

Maybe I can be a full-time teacher somewhere.

At a school.

Or a small college.

When I can ensure them some sort of stability, I will tell them everything, the quitting of the PhD, my next steps. I need more time to figure this out, and once I do, I will tell them everything.

Half of me says, By not telling the truth, you only hurt yourself. And the other half says, But by tell-ing the truth now, without a plan of how to proceed, you will hurt them more. What would telling them accomplish? It will only cause strife.

Peace of mind? Encouragement? Support?

Don't say catharsis.

Catharsis.

I don't want to get married until I have done more for myself. But also I owe it to them to do more for myself, which is what Eric didn't understand; he said, You shouldn't owe them anything. We argue over this. The American brings up the individual. The Chinese brings up *xiao shun*. When I ask Eric if he thinks a child can ever feel entirely independent of her parents, he says, What kind of question is that?

But now I don't really know. There is too much already shared.

Mother, Father, I think I know what it means to hurt for you.

.   .   .

A strange thing happens when the best friend takes the aluminum heart to counseling. She sets it on the table and the table is no longer covered in flames. There is also less yelling.

So she takes it every week and sets it on the table.

Finally, she says, the room is just a room and she can properly see his face as she had remembered it.

When I am visiting them at their condo, she gives me her reasons:

We make a good team. We are financially very stable. The child will have a good life. Also, she has been thinking more about the beginning. The person she married is still in there.

But what about you? I ask, while the husband and baby are in the other room.

What about me?

You won't be entirely happy.

That's possible.

But then we hear the baby shriek in the other room and run in.

Is the baby all right? Is something the matter?

Everything is fine.

Except the husband has found another thing that makes her laugh in that paper-shredding way. It is just him standing there, touching his nose.

.   .   .

In a letter to his daughter, Einstein wrote that love is the only energy in the universe that man has not learned to drive at will. He posited it to be the universal force scientists have overlooked.

Even if Eric did not always understand, his devotion to me, how did I miss that? Logically I think I knew but I needed to hear someone else say it first.

The jump he once spoke about is what I keep coming back to. How he was able to do it and I was not.

To progress in life, you must always compare yourself with someone better.

Maybe not better in all aspects but better in some.

I watch him wade into the river first and he could

keep going. But he stops in the middle of the current and waits for me to catch up.

. . .

A sunny weekend. A warm breeze. For two weeks in July, there are no complaints about the weather.

I am hosting a very small dinner party. The baby has turned one, so I have strung up banners and filled a piñata and fastened, to the best of my abilities, a party hat on the dog, who is so frightened by the hat that he has hidden away in the closet, teeth chattering.

The best friend and husband are here. The math student. We watch the baby play with her toys.

Don't say toys, the best friend whispers. Say friends. She knows. I don't know how she knows, she just does.

So we watch her throw her friends from one corner of the room to the other, then line them up in a row by size and scold them.

Baa bee woo, baa bee woo.

This baby might very well be a genius. She is also so coy and wiggles her pinkie at the person she's never met before, the math student. Come hither, says the genius pinkie. I wish to be pushed in my stroller throne.

He goes while the husband stands close to the best friend as if held to her by rubber bands. A few feet of space and he will wince from pain.

How can I help? What can I do? The husband asks many questions.

Finally, we send him to the store for cheddar cheese. He comes back having bought every kind of cheddar cheese at the store. I have to laugh. What are we going to do with this much cheese? Our three-cheese dip must now quadruple.

While making this dip, I pull the best friend aside. So? I say, motioning to the math student, who is still pushing the stroller but now making train sounds.

He is a very good train, she says. Probably the best I have seen. But your guess is as good as mine.

I'd rather not guess.

. . .

It was once believed that heart cells could not regenerate, that once they died they could not be replaced. Now it is known that the heart can renew itself. But the process is very slow. In an average person, the rate is 1 percent each year.

Eric's new lab has a web page and this web page has pictures. One picture is of Eric with his arm around another woman and it has got me refreshing the page nonstop.

Who is this woman and where did she come from and what is her age, height, weight, family history, and pet preference? Where are the words that go along with this picture? I need a thousand or so. Let me google her. But at this moment, Google chooses to be slow and shitty and unhelpful.

She is another faculty member, I discover. Also in

chemistry. She has a list of publications so long that when I scroll to the bottom, there is a button that says next.

Next is overrated, I say to the dog.

Here is me not clicking next. Here is me closing out of the web page. Here is me reopening the web page, clicking next, and then telling the dog, Not a word to anybody, not even to your squirrel friends.

Another bet: If tomorrow the world comes to an end, I will e-mail Eric about this woman. If not, then I will forget about it.

The Big Crunch is what they call the end of the universe, should it collapse back on itself again. Currently, this is just speculation, but billions of years down the line, we will know for sure. If humans are still around for the Big Crunch, they will surely panic. They will run to the supermarkets and buy out all the water.

I spend a whole session talking to the shrink about the Big Crunch and then I mention how I am worried that the dog has too many girlfriends. He has at least five girlfriends in the neighborhood, all pugs.

. . .

What kind of flowers do you like? asks the math student.

Not roses or large arrangements. Nothing too cluttered or perfect looking.

Soon, I get a delivery of potted grass.

Um, says the delivery boy.

It is magnificent, I reply.

At the park, I flick the petals of every flower I see.

You might be a child, Eric said, whenever he saw me do that. Then the peck to the forehead, the spot where my fingers are now rubbing.

When the math student and I kiss, there is no teeth clanking. It is well executed.

He tells me the potted grass was a surprise birthday present.

But you are three months ahead of schedule.

He says, had he given it to me on my actual birthday, it would not have been a surprise.

.   .   .

The world has not come to an end. So I guess I will forget about her, the woman in the picture. What were the chances that she would be both good-looking and brilliant? Why couldn't it have been just one or the other? She might be too tall for him though. They are at eye level. He cannot rest his chin on top of her head.

But perhaps women like her don't need chins resting on their heads.

.   .   .

Chinese is actually quite musical. When I told Eric that, it surprised him.

The four great Chinese novels are *Water Margin, Dream of the Red Chamber, Romance of the Three Kingdoms,* and *Journey to the West.*

When I first heard these titles, I cringed. In translation, much of the cadence was lost. *Journey to the West* is *Xi You Ji,* three syllables, very punchy. This novel is my favorite. It is an adventure novel about a band of misfit companions traveling across China fighting evil. The hero is the Monkey King. He is a half-god, half-monkey being who pulls from his ear a baton that can grow into any size and smite enemies. But he is not a perfect hero. Most of the time, he is a rebel. Hence why his closest companion is a monk who is pure of heart.

My mother: If you are going to read a Chinese novel, let it be that one.

I think it is because this novel is the most fun, the characters larger than life. But now I wonder. Maybe it is also to remind me that such a hero exists in our culture. A Monkey King instead of a sheep.

About the novel, I had told Eric, The monk reminds me a lot of you. Except that he was always chanting prayers and you are always humming tunes.

Where is home for you? the shrink asks.

I'm not sure. Does it matter? I like being in between places for the time being.

For my mother, I know exactly where she would consider home. Home is where her mother is.

My father, I had always assumed, does not deal in these abstract matters.

But then why does this memory come back to me?

I am a child who is prone to motion sickness and never likes riding in cars.

My father's remedy for motion sickness is to look at green things in the distance. Look at that hill, he says, or that batch of trees. To this day, I have not heard anyone else say that. I have heard of looking at stationary objects in the distance, but never the green.

Then I visit the place where he grew up. I do not realize it then—I am too young—but I realize it now. In the distance, on all sides, was green.

. . .

A day of doing nothing, except playing fetch with the dog. The next day, I tell the shrink, If you ever smell the dog's fur you will know what the sun smells like. Like toasted corn chips.

. . .

There is a pretty good proposal in *Stepmom*. The man ties a string to the woman's finger and then slides a ring down that string. He says he had let the string break once but he would not let it break again.

When proposing to my mother, my father wraps a

blade of grass around her finger. They are visiting his family in the countryside. She rides with him on his bike, hands around his waist. The bike hits a bump and they both fall into the dirt. She arrives at his home filthy but not unhappy. Dirt washes off, she says, and he realizes then that she is not as delicate as she looks. Still a student, he is too poor to afford a ring, but, while wrapping the grass around her finger, he says that in the future he will make her one himself.

My father goes on to become a specialist in metal alloys. The year before I leave for college, he makes her a ring out of iron, tungsten, molybdenum, chromium, and titanium. He calibrates the proportions himself and then melts down the elements and then molds the ring in his laboratory, to the exact size of her finger. A size three finger.

I watch my mother take the ring out of the plastic bag and hold it up to the light.

Of the alloy, my father says that it is strong. He says that it will bend before it will break.

My mother, who is never at a loss for words, is at a loss for words.

For a long time, scientists did not know why the nucleus of an atom held together. Theoretically, it should not. It is made up of all positive charges that should repel, but somehow, it persists.

I do not think she would have ever stepped out of that car. I think by the count of three, she would have stopped.

Eventually, she says to him, Whatever happens, no divorce.

. . .

On my actual birthday, I receive a handful of cards. Most from faraway friends. Two from the best friend. But there is one that catches me off guard. I look down and immediately know the handwriting. All lowercase. The *n*s that look like *r*s, the *r*s that look like *s*s.

I had frequently said of his handwriting, Not even Alan Turing could decipher it.

He jokes, *You are now very old in dog years.*

He says, *Ohio is very flat.*

I notice tiny dots in places where nothing is written. I wonder if these are where he put down his pen and then lifted it back up, thinking of something else to say.

After the second time he asked, Eric said, I could not have been with you for so long had I not also considered you my equal. But what was so great about being an equal, I thought, when in the end, all marriages are doomed?

I now ask the best friend, Tell me again why you're staying with him?

A very good team. Financially stable. The nose touching.

Yes, the nose touching.

. . .

Two marriages:

Clara and Fritz Haber: Clara finishes a doctorate in chemistry. She is the only woman at her school. She is brilliant but reserved. The first time Fritz proposes, she declines. The second time, she agrees. After they marry, he demands that Clara be a housewife and a mother, while he travels for work. When war breaks out in 1918, he proves his patriotism through the development of a new weapon, something invisible to the human eye and absolutely silent. After finding out about the chlorine gas, Clara shoots herself in the family garden.

Marie and Pierre Curie: Pierre makes several marriage proposals to Marie before she accepts. A commonality then between these women. On her wedding day, she wears a dark blue dress. More practical, she thinks, and afterward, in her dress, goes back to the laboratory with Pierre. The lab is the basement of their home. In three years, they discover polonium and radium. In eight, they are awarded a Nobel. At first the committee will not recognize her (no woman has won before) but Pierre demands it—she is the one who sifted through ten tons of mineral-rich ore to find that tenth of a gram.

———

It might be that all marriages lie between these two extremes.

When the wave-particle duality is first proposed, there is a shift in scientific thinking. Before then, everything is thought to be known. Afterward, Heisenberg's uncertainty principle develops. Schrödinger and his cat.

. . .

Eric, I have hurt for you too.

A few years ago, my mother went back to China to visit her mother. They sent over a box of sweets that were my childhood favorites. I ate my way through the box and then stopped at the last piece. I couldn't bring myself to eat it. Too precious, I thought. I left it on the counter and watched it slowly grow mold. Even when you said, This needs to go, I refused. I put the piece into a plastic container and then in the back of the fridge. On the day that you left, I took the piece out and ate it. Then I got sick for eleven days.

Pure crystals are those that have perfectly repeating units. You told me this after I asked you what you found beautiful about chemistry. But what of the repeating units in life? Most often imperfect.

Eric, I am writing you a short note. I am asking: *Would you ever consider coming back and visiting for a little while, just as a friend?*

ACKNOWLEDGMENTS

Thanks to my incredible BU writing teachers Leslie, Xuefei, and Sigrid for guiding me through my MFA year and beyond. Thanks to my exceptionally hardworking writing cohort Jamie, Caroline, Jeff, Michael M, Zoe, Jillian, Michelle, Katie, and Leigh for helping me revise this manuscript to the best that it could be. Thanks to Jamie, Caroline, Jeff, Michael M, and Catherine for their continual support over phone, e-mail, and the occasional night out. Thanks to Michael C for being my first and last reader. Thanks to Linda and Yuying for their extraordinary years of friendship. Thanks to Joy for believing in this work and me. Thanks to Jennifer for her insights, edits, and words of encouragement. Thanks to everyone at Knopf for making this novel possible. Thanks to my earliest writing teacher and mentor, Amy, for encouraging me to write in the first place. Thanks especially to my parents.

A NOTE ABOUT THE AUTHOR

WEIKE WANG is a graduate of Harvard University, where she earned her undergraduate degree in chemistry and her doctorate in public health. She received her MFA from Boston University. Her fiction has been published in literary magazines including *Alaska Quarterly Review, Glimmer Train,* and *Ploughshares*. She currently lives in New York City, and *Chemistry* is her first novel.

A NOTE ON THE TYPE

This book was set in Granjon, a type named in compliment to Robert Granjon, a type cutter and printer active in Antwerp, Lyons, Rome, and Paris from 1523 to 1590.

Linotype Granjon was designed by George W. Jones, who based his drawings on a face used by Claude Garamond (ca. 1480–1561) in his beautiful French books. Granjon more closely resembles Garamond's own type than do any of the various modern faces that bear his name.

Typeset by Scribe,
Philadelphia, Pennsylvania

Printed and bound by Berryville Graphics,
Berryville, Virginia

Designed by Cassandra J. Pappas